Okafor Meets his Match and Other Stories

Okafor Meets his Match and Other Stories

Richard C. Kumengisa

SPEARS
MEDIA PRESS

Also by Richard C. Kumengisa

NOVELS
The Odour of Death
The Legacy
The Gun

RADIO PLAYS
Singer of an Old Song
Bananas
For the Dead

SHORT STORIES
Zow and the Village Belle
Mati wun
The Witchdoctor
The Warder's Assignment
Leopard Killer
The Last Hunt
The Brief Stop

SPEARS MEDIA PRESS

Denver • Bamenda

7830 W. Alameda Ave, Suite 103 Denver, CO 80226

Anembom Consulting Building, Cow Street, Bamenda

P O Box 1151, Bamenda, NWR, Cameroon

Spears Media Press publishes under the auspices of the Spears Media Association.

The Press furthers the Association's mission by advancing knowledge in education, learning, entertainment and research.

First Published 2016 by Spears Media Press
www.spearsmedia.com
info@spearsmedia.com
Information on this title: www.spearsmedia.com/shortstories
© Richard C. Kumengisa 2016
All rights reserved.

Ordering Information:
Special discounts are available on bulk purchases by corporations, associations, and others. For details, contact the publisher at any of the addresses above.

ISBN: 978-1-942876-06-9 [Paperback]
ISBN: 978-1-942876-03-8 [Ebook]

In loving memory of
Dr. Herman B. Maimo,
Fai wo Bamfem
and to the courage and togetherness of the Nso people
among whom I count many a friend.

Contents

Okafor Meets his Match

INTRODUCTION

The idea behind the short story "Okafor Meets his Match" is to recapture the kaleidoscope of the last days of colonisation in Banso in particular and Southern Cameroon in general through an amusing narration.

Some history is brought in to prick the reader's curiosity and a few vocabulary items and expressions are thrown in to enhance English. It is obvious that Ngong and Okafor are from different linguistic and socio-cultural backgrounds from the way they speak and act.

For a short story, "Okafor Meets his Match" is very ambitious. It touches the economic, social and psychological oppression Eastern Nigerians secretly meted out on the people of this part of the country under the very noses of their British colonial masters.

Matters reached a peak in Kumbo when a brutalized Banso man accepted the challenge of a fight from an Ibo trader in the marketplace. The result of the fight would be of great importance in the land.

The Ibos thought the trader, Okafor, would easily win the fight since boxing was their thing and he was known to be good at it. The Banso man, Ngong, was ready for the event with his native style of fighting.

During the fight, the Bansos were scared and disappointed

by the clumsiness and apparent stupidity of their tribesman. The Ibos were boastful and praised their man loudly. As for Ngong, he played the fool to the great annoyance of the Bansos, until the very end when he knocked down his adversary.

The Bansos carried their victor shoulder high and the traditional dance of Captain Umaru Ngong materialized from nowhere for the spontaneous celebration of Ngong's victory in typical dance and drink, as the joyous group headed for the nearest "shah" house.

The Fon would hear of Ngong's feat and give him a red feather in his cap for liberating his tribe from bondage. Henceforth the Ibos would be apprehensive of any wrong they wanted to do to the Bansos. Peace would reign.

RCK

CHAPTER ONE

Our part of the country suffered a double colonisation up to 1961 when it had independence. Great Britain ruled us, a U.N. trusteeship territory, as a part of Eastern Nigeria. That was the obvious, the main and the milder part of our twin colonisations.

The subtle and more terrible was the colonisation within that colonisation. It was from the people of the aforementioned Eastern Nigeria. They were mostly Ibos and a few Effiks resident in Bamenda Province and most of the then Southern Cameroons.

Thus independence celebrations for us were not only because of political liberation from the white man but also because of freedom from economic oppression from our own kind.

In those days Ibos regarded us as primitive second-class citizens, good for little else but exploitation and bullying. They thought we had no notion of economy in our private lives even though we were extremely poor.

Our masters by assertion took pleasure in making fun of the extravagant way that, they said, we ate *garri and okra sauce*, a very popular meal in Eastern Nigeria.

They let it be known that we made a poor show of it. Instead of making lumps the size of table tennis balls out of the garri, letting these barely touch the okra sauce and then swallowing them without letting our teeth as much as touch them, we went the foolish, wasteful way.

We would make balls all right. Then stupidly make deep depressions in them with our thumbs, fill these with okra sauce, toss them into our mouths and finally worsen matters by chewing the mouthfuls as if we were all old toothless people revisiting their abandoned chewing habit with such soft material.

They had nice times telling each other what spendthrifts Southern Cameroonians were. Those people lived for the day and never thought of the next.

Only four of them would finish a whole bottle of beer! They ate and made merry each day as if it was their very last here on earth. They were number one on the list of Epicureans in the modern world.

"Nna, unu Cameloon," they would say complacently, "Unu no gettu no small sensu. Looku wetin unu dey do. Taku garre turn canoe for carry okro soupu inside. Ah be wetin unu go choppu tomorrow, eh? Chineke!"

Freely translated into English, it would be: "Fellow, you Cameroonians don't have the least sense. Look at what you do. You make a canoe out of garri in which to carry okra sauce. By gully, what will you eat tomorrow? God!"

One would imagine them eating in special local restaurants where meals went for very low prices. They would order garri and okra sauce "without no meat but with plenty *particulars*".

They always made it very clear that if the waiter served them meat, he would pay for it out of his own pocket.

Particulars were tiny bits of smoked fish and crayfish used for seasoning the okra sauce. They had an indefinite taste and were served free. A piece of meat or fish had a separate charge.

Eastern Nigerians could afford to laugh at us despite their comically austere way of life because their people were in powerful posts of responsibility in the offices of our other colonial lords.

For fear of repercussions our parents neither expressed their dissatisfaction nor derided them back in any way. So the black colonialists did as they liked most of the time. They could do and undo. What they wanted they took.

The worst part of our chastisement was in the marketplace where Ibos had given themselves a monopoly for the sale of cloth and a good number of other imported goods with an inelastic demand.

Our people were relegated to wood, charcoal and locally produced foodstuff. Very few had the money or the nerve to compete with the aliens.

When a Southern Cameroonian asked the price of a length of cloth in an Ibo man's stall in the market, the seller would, without saying a word, simply cut off the quantity of cloth mentioned and give his underling a price.

The latter would be compelled to buy it at the former's charge or face drastic consequences.

Asking the price of anything from an Ibo man in the market was tantamount to buying it for the Southern Cameroonian. Woe betides him if he dared refuse to buy a thing after asking the price.

The sounds of the beating tambourines would fill the marketplace. That was the sign for rallying all Ibos.

An unequal fight would ensue and, as the Ibos had a heinous esprit de corps, a good number of them would together beat up the would-be buyer to within an inch of death. The others would watch and make scathing comments to further punish their victim.

The headstrong person would thus learn how to buy as they prescribed and would still be made to buy the source of trouble.

"Taku garre turn canoe…"

Reality for us was: when you asked for the price of a thing from an Ibo trader, he told you and you bought it at the price you had been told without demur. Most market-goers knew this rule and obeyed it.

Bargaining was out of question. This, in a society where lengthy bargaining was, and still is, part and parcel of the buying and selling process, the part, in fact, that embellishes it.

Certain places were exception to this rule in the Province.

The Nso area, in general, and Kumbo, its headquarters, in particular, were typical examples.

It may have been because the people there were more widely travelled through their trade in kola nuts and tobacco with Northern Nigeria. Or, perhaps, they were naturally more aware and assertive of their rights.

At the beginning of the colonial era, the Germans, despite their vastly superior weaponry, had found the Bansos a difficult people to vanquish.

They were one of the most powerful and populous tribes in the province and through love of their stratified society and adoration of a deep-rooted language and culture, they had forged themselves a respected place not only in the province but also in the country.

If the Ibos had heard the story of the war with the Germans or were aware of the stature of the Bansos, none of these had impressed them. They were hidebound and needed a lesson to tell them where they were and with whom they were dealing.

It took a single fight which so shocked them that even till today, with an excellent relationship between Cameroon and Nigeria, the population of Ibos in Banso is very scanty and extremely wary of provoking the Nso man to anger.

The event was not planned. It came as a result of a people pushing their advantage too far in a neighbourhood that was not theirs and getting the opposite of what they expected.

Some people can take oppression more easily than others. The Ibos met with a people to whom life was equal to freedom. Without it they would rather not live.

The story that follows shows what was typical of the Nso man. His posterity is still possessed of the same spirit. It runs in their blood.

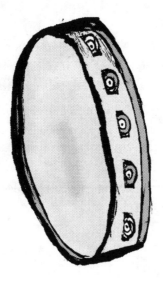

A tambourine

CHAPTER TWO

Ngong Wirkikai was a placid, non-trouble-seeking Kumbo man who, in a warm mid-afternoon in the dry season, set out for the Kumbo Market from Bamfem, where he lived, to buy a special piece of cloth for his expecting wife. She had insisted on a particular colour and design and he wanted to make her happy.

At the marketplace he accosted an Ibo trader by name John Okafor. He politely wished to know how much a fathom of the cloth he was pointing at would cost. It was not quite what his wife had described but it was close. It would do.

"How much for that one," he asked in his broad Banso accent.

Instead of telling him the price, the Ibo man quickly cut off one fathom of the material, folded it and made it into a neat rectangular package in a cellophane bag.

This he thrust, with an expression of finality on his face, into the unsuspecting hands of Ngong Wirkikai who caught it before realising the meaning of what he was doing.

Ngong had heard of the trick but he had never thought it would be used on him some day. He tried to smile the matter off but irritation at the unfair treatment held the smile back.

He patiently asked John Okafor how much he wanted him to pay for the cloth. If there was little ado about the matter, he might as well buy the cloth and take it home to his wife.

Okafor told him a price that was three times what he had expected.

"Nna you must give me theree pounds one times for dat cloth whe you don make ah cuttam," he said.

Ngong was scandalized.

"Master, nyamu," he told the Ibo trader, "all my wealth in the world is nowhere near what you want. I think I'd rather try somewhere else."

He thought his wife would have to do without that type of cloth if it cost such a fortune.

He put the package on Okafor's stool and was turning away when the trader gave him a quick slap on each cheek. The two exploded like two pistol shots fired in quick succession.

Okafor looked angrily into Ngong's eyes.

"Don'tu be stupidi," he said. "Ah be na you buy di cloth give me for sellam nko."

Ngong Wirkikai's cheeks were burning. He cocked his head to one side as if listening intently to what Okafor would say next. He was feeling the sting of the slaps on both cheeks as he carefully arranged the package on the trader's stool.

He looked up and demanded an explanation. No tribesman of his had ever struck him like that, let alone a foreigner. He did not think he looked like anybody's wife.

"Yumi! yumi! yumi! Master," he exclaimed in his native Lamnso. "Abai, you must tell me what wrong I've done to merit your slaps."

"Don'tu open your mautu talk here," the Ibo trader retorted. "You make me ah cuttu my cloth, you don'tu want to buy. Ah bi na you gettu dis muarketi, eh? Just pay my money, theree pounds ten shellengs, taku your cloth go jari. No jus try talku again or – looku ah no sabby talku plenty, eh."

Ngong ignored the threat and the increase in price. He

folded his arms across his chest. His determination to get to the bottom of the matter was written all over his tense body. Yet his humility was greater than his anger.

"Please, Master, do tell me why you've slapped me," he continued. "As you see me, I'm one who doesn't like trouble. Please, tell me."

"Looku," the trader continued, "Ah no go leggo you when you never pay my money."

The trader gripped Ngong at the neck of the *danchiki* and tried to pull him farther into the store. He found the Kumbo man an immovable rock.

When Ngong knocked the pulling hands from his body, the Ibo man quickly stepped back, went into the Western boxing stance, and beckoned him.

Both his fists were clenched, with the right one almost touching his chin and the left some six inches in front of the former. His body was turned sideways with the left foot a step in front of the right and he was arched forward. There indeed was the perfect picture of a boxing champion.

He wore a black T-shirt with two red lines across the chest. His trousers were gray with large silver side buckles to hold them in place. His feet were shod in the sports shoes in vogue: black with white tongues and heels.

In dress, physique and skill the Eastern Nigerian was ready for anything out of anywhere in the world.

Ngong Wirkikai looked at the foreigner and shook his head. Was that how far the Ibo man would go? He squared his shoulders and he too stepped back into a traditional fighting posture.

He clenched his right fist and hid it away in the small of his back with the back of his hand touching his striped red and black *danchiki* and his elbow bent tightly.

Then he thrust his left foot forward and held up his left arm with its clenched fist in front of him like a shield.

Ngong's danchiki was embroidered in blue at the neck. His short baggy trousers were maroon and did not reach his ankles. Below these were his "motor foot" shoes with uppers made from the inner tube of a car tyre and the soles cut from a worn tyre. They were covered with a layer of fine brown dust from the road to Bamfem, the *faidom* he had moved into from his native Kikaikilaiki, Kay Four, after marriage.

The two men stood there, looking into each other's eyes like two cocks about to start fighting. From each was the unvoiced statement "I can beat you".

Word of what was happening had quickly gone round the Ibo stalls in the marketplace. Their drummers had forgotten to beat the rallying tambourines. Yet the Ibos came out with eyes narrowed in anger. Which loafer of a Southern Cameroonian had dared stand against an Ibo man? He would get it hot.

Bansos swarmed into the area. Everybody wanted to watch. The ensuing fight would be the first of its kind in the land.

The Ibos were confident of the boxing skill of their tribes-man. The two men were of about the same build and height but the Kumbo man was more muscular.

Their man's arms were longer and they knew the reach to be a great advantage in boxing. He would keep the native at bay and give him hot pepper-soup to drink.

Of course the Nso fellow was no match for their man. Muscles with no skill were no use in a fight. And those muscles might be as soft as freshly dug clay.

They certainly would not need to give Okafor a helping hand. He would teach the Nso fool a lesson. Let them start the combat. The end of the native was at hand.

The Bansos were apprehensive. Ibos were good fighters.

This one was showing proof of great skill in boxing, that great thing of the white man's martial art. He would be able to throw hard blows with a great deal of speed, deadly accuracy and ease. They were scared.

They had to do something to save their tribesman. It was better for them to arrest the situation before Ngong was demolished and made to eat dirt in the land of his forefathers who had fought the Germans bravely and in front of his tribesmen and foreigners together

Most of the humiliation would rub off on them and they would pay dearly all round to the Ibos.

They tried to lay hands on Ngong to restrain him. As they approached, Ngong Wirkikai turned towards them. His face was distorted with cold anger. If looks could kill, Ngong would have killed the lot of them with the hard look on his face.

He shook his muscular shoulders before they could touch him. So they left him alone. He had chosen to prepare for his funeral himself. Who were they to stop him from his choice?

They would be there to take the spade from his hands after he had finished digging his own grave and entered it.

They thought they might succeed with the Ibo trader. They tried to grab him but he danced round on the balls of his feet and threw a few quick jabs in the air at them.

They stepped back. They knew how devastating Western boxing could be. The Ibo man was master of it. None of them wanted to stop the first blow from the powerful fighting machine.

The perfect picture of a boxing champion.

CHAPTER THREE

Before they even gave up trying to stop the Ibo trader, Ngong Wirkikai had begun repeating: *"Mati wun, mati wun, mati wun,"* – "Leave him alone, leave him alone, leave him alone."

Each time he said it, he would raise his left arm above his forehead as if parrying a blow and bring it back down in front of his nose, taking a step forward simultaneously.

John Okafor knew exactly what he was going to do. Only once did he speak after taking his impressive fighting stance. This was business and there was no use wasting time on empty words.

"Nna, unu leavam. Unu leavam," said he, "make ah showam somethins, make ah broke dat him big mautu whe e de talku witham. Make ah lockam one times."

The two men advanced on each other. John Okafor suddenly started raining blows on Ngong's face, chest and belly. The blows were quick but fairly light.

The Bansos held their breath while the Ibos began cheering and praising their own man for his skill. He went on throwing punches like the boxing machine he was thought to be. Ngong was taking them calmly.

The Bansos marvelled. When the Ibo man would be done, they would have nothing left but the pieces of their man. He would get what he had insisted on getting: disgrace for himself and the whole tribe.

"Mati wun, mati wun, mati wun."

They were there to watch him make a fool of himself. Let him go ahead since he knew more than everyone else!

The blows did not move Ngong back. Okafor was winning the fight right from the beginning. But it was he who was retreating steadily and not his victim who was moving forward rhythmically with inflexible determination punctuated by the monotonous "mati wun, mati wun, mati wun".

Ngong's "mati wun, mati wun" was now accompanied by a much firmer step forward with the left foot followed by another with the right.

The shield arm that had brushed aside a good number of blows from his body disturbed the Ibo pugilist. It felt like iron whenever he made contact with it.

He feared any blow from its hand and feared even more a blow from the hidden one. He was sure that right arm would be pure steel.

He doubled the rate of delivery of his punches. He had to knock down the fool quickly and get onto more important business.

The Ibos went on with their cheers and noisy encouragement of their man and provocative calls to the Nso fighter.

"Downam Hogan King Bassey," one said, referring to their famous Nigerian featherweight champion of the whole world.

"Remember your poisonous left hand Hogan King Bassey," another one chimed in.

"Okafor!" a rough voice shouted. "Dat one na butter. Takam choppu your bread."

The Kumbo man did not look round.

"Mati wun, mati wun, mati wun" came his determined, monotonous, unique utterance.

He received a left hook on the right ear and a light upper-cut on his Adam's apple. He was annoyed with himself for not having been fast enough to take all the blows on his shield arm. He knew yielding to anger in a fight would be suicidal, so he controlled his.

When he got a particularly hard blow on the mouth, he put the fingertips of his left hand to his lips, looked at them while Okafor danced stylishly round him, and saw blood. That was blood from inside him. His blood drawn by a foreigner! In his fatherland!

He got mad.

"Aha!" he cried and stepped back quickly.

The Bansos thought the moment of reaction from Ngong Wirkikai had come. He would prove himself the Nso man that he ought to be.

They waited anxiously. They were disappointed. The Kumbo man stuck his head between his thick shoulders and the now annoying "mati wun, mati wun, mati wun" kept dropping from his mouth like beans from a badly constructed barn.

His heavy left foot kept stepping forward and his clumsy right one would drag after it, as if in mocking pursuit, leaving tyre marks from his soles on the dusty ground.

Okafor boxed harder. With agility he connected a good number of left and right hooks. Then he missed a wild upper-cut but followed with combinations to his opponent's breast and head.

Left right, left right, left right the blows landed on Ngong Wirkikai as if on a punching bag. He took most of them on his left arm. The others crashed into their target – his body.

He did not seem to feel them and stayed indifferent to the punishment he was receiving. His tribesmen felt like eating him alive.

The Ibos were now jumping about in an uncommon frenzy of happiness. A few of them stuck their tongues out at the miserable Bansos around. Others jeered and booed.

Okafor was sweating on his nose. To the Ibos, it was the sweat of victory. They cheered even louder and a few of them began to dance the Twist while others did the Highlife. Ngong remained unperturbed.

The Bansos had gone completely dumb. "Mati wun, mati wun, mati wun" was no more coming from Ngong's mouth. His squat head was stuck deeper in his chest. His footwork went on in pantomime. His tribesmen watched him with utter disgust.

Had they the chance, despite the odds, most of them would have liked to take Ngong's place in the fight to show him how a man, a real man, a man from Nso fought.

Ngong was not fighting. He was being beaten right there in front of his tribesmen, in the main market of his home area.

Ngong had taken scores of blows outside those he had brushed aside with his useless muscular shield arm but had not delivered a single one. He ought to give back just one blow to save his honour, to show the Ibos that no Nso man was useless in a fight.

He would not. He had gone far enough. What was he waiting for? The Ibo man would soon knock him down. He was wearing the moron down for the kill.

...began to dance the Twist while others did the Highlife.

CHAPTER FOUR

Ngong was chasing Okafor round and round in circles within the space in front of the latter's store but it was Okafor who was delivering the blows all the time.

It was also Okafor who was beginning to show signs of weariness. His blows were becoming lighter and slower.

Ngong's energy might just possibly still be all there while Okafor's was half-drained in rapid action. That could not be so for a right thinking man should not die of thirst with a cauldron of water by his side. Only a fool would and Ngong was proving to be a big one.

It was a matter of time before the battle would be over in favour of the Ibo man. The little intelligence and strength Ngong had left were for running round and round after his opponent.

The pride of Nso would soon be at ground level. How would the Fon react to the news? What would all Nso think?

There would also be Ngong's pregnant wife to bear the disgraceful news of the easy defeat of the man she had married, if man he really was.

The Bansos were so miserable that they looked like hungry neglected orphans in an African war of genocide.

A few of them had developed such antipathy for Ngong that, in their frustration, they would have liked to cheer and dance along with the Ibos but dared not go that far.

Then one of the boisterous aliens, a flat-nosed clumsy-looking sexagenarian with an amorphous brown old bowler hat on his gray-haired boulder of a head, stuck his pink tongue out of his wide snail-eating mouth and was nodding like a naughty child showing off sweets to its less fortunate friends.

The expression on the faces of the Kumbo men betrayed their thoughts. Ngong was a hateful idiot to make them suffer that much pain.

Ngong looked round briefly at the derisive large pink tongue of the fat headed Ibo. Then he suddenly felt the fist in the small of his back. He brushed aside a tornado of blows.

Now the killer in him surfaced.

He looked at Okafor with an eagle's eye. For the first time since the beginning of the fight, real excitement showed on his taciturn countenance.

He took two short steps back and Okafor took a long one in pursuit. The trader was confident. He was too much so. That step forward was his undoing.

Ngong's lips moved as he murmured something in Lamso to his ancestors and momentarily closed his eyes.

Then he made his move. He leaned slightly right. John Okafor had been delivering blows for too long to reckon with reception. He was indifferent to the significance of his adversary's body movement.

When Ngong unleashed the blow he had been hiding since the beginning of the fight, the devastating "nkuum Nso" of the Bansos, the blow of blows, it connected with a thud like a bamboo striking the stem of a banana plant.

The result was terrible.

Okafor was caught completely off guard. The blow landed on his left temple and his dancing legs refused to dance and turned to butter. His weight was too much now for the weakened legs.

He stood dazed for a split second; then he crashed to the dusty ground like a log of Mendandwe charcoal wood tree.

The whites of his eyes showed briefly and he closed the eyes tightly and grimaced in pain.

His face sagged and blood began to spout from his nose and mouth. It trickled to the ground that was crisscrossed with tyre marks from Ngong's soles interwoven with prints from Okafor's sports shoes.

The watching Ibos shrieked in disbelief, humiliation and dismay. Behind Ngong the sexagenarian pink tongue had disappeared into the big mouth whose thick lips hung open. Brown teeth showed between them.

The cheering and dancing had stopped. Deep silence and momentary inactivity had imposed themselves on the scene.

Ngong stood there ready, waiting for the trader to stand up and fight. Or did the fellow prefer to continue from the ground? "So be it," the expression on the Kumbo man's face seemed to say.

He was on the balls of his feet, swaying forwards and backwards like a short tree in the wind. He was ready for more action.

Suddenly he sprang forward and took his native fighting stance anew. "Mati wun, mati wun, mati wun" came from between his bruised and slightly swollen lips with the same old monotony but now with a relieving effect on his watching tribesmen.

Ngong suddenly bent over the stunned and bleeding Okafor on the ground and raised his glistening vibrating right fist into his armpit to crash it into the bleeding face of his adversary.

The muscles of his cheeks were trembling. There was murder in his eyes. His intention was obvious. He wanted to finish the fight his way.

His people had the common sense to step forward and seize him before he went too far. The warrior had proven himself a true son of Nso. There was nothing to strive for. The fight was ended.

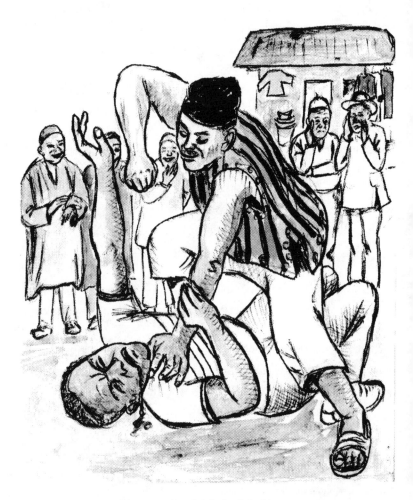

He wanted to finish the fight his way.

Nso had won the day but the Bansos feared for the life of the Eastern Nigerian. If he died, his compatriots would have a completely different story to tell their fellow countrymen in the police force and legal department.

There was shock on the faces of the erstwhile cheering Ibos. Two times did Okafor try to get up but fell back to the ground.

His supporters, with their heads bowed, watched him for a while in disappointment and humiliation, then picked him up and carried him away to seek first aid.

A trail of blood from the defeated fighter's mouth kept abreast with them as they hurried away. It was really a hard blow they had been struck.

It was a mean trick fate had played on them despite the many advantages they had had. Their man had been winning all the time. He was clearly the better fighter. Yet he had lost so woefully.

CHAPTER FIVE

The result of the fight would change a great deal in the relationship between the Bansos and themselves. They had lost their superior position.

Many Nso people would follow Ngong Wirkikai's example. The fight had drawn a line. Henceforth, if they tried anything the Bansos did not think was correct, they would have the devil to pay.

They suffered the misery of the defeated proud. A few of them began to give serious thought to leaving the Nso area altogether.

There was really no need for that because the Bansos had made their point and were not about to start a chapter of persecution of their fellow Africans.

If Ngong had missed, or if Okafor had dodged the blow, the Kumbo man would have crashed to the ground, carried by the momentum of his swing.

Luckily Okafor had been taken unawares and Ngong had not missed with his native blow, the "nkuum Nso".

Seeing that the Ibo man was only wounded, the Bansos joyfully carried Ngong Wirkikai on their shoulders. That did not stop him from spitting out his last "mati wun, mati wun, mati wun" before it finally dawned on him that the fight was over. He was the victor.

His face brightened up in a broad smile. He was a real man,

a real Nso man. Satisfaction showed on his once more placid countenance. He would rather have died than let a soldier of a foreign army defeat him in the land of his forebears.

He glanced at the source of all the trouble. It was still there where he had left it – on top of John Okafor's stool. Let it stay where it was.

The Bansos who carried Ngong Wirkikai were gingerly placing him at the threshold of the nearest *shah* bar when *Mbaya* music broke out behind them.

It was Captain Umaru Ngong's Mbaya Dance Group which had suddenly appeared, from where only God knew, for the celebration of Ngong Wirkikai's victory.

The dancers became the centre of attention. Their song about the roasted yam was making everybody dance with head and toe. They soon formed a circle with the captain in command and his dancers stepping out into the middle in turns to show off their styles.

They all would celebrate the cherished victory of their liberation over calabashes of corn brew and in Captain Ngong's hot music and dance and might only go back home late in the evening drunk but happy.

The Nso early afternoon sun was shining directly and warmly down on them as they made merry.

The palace would hear about the fit. So would *Nwerong* who would give Ngong Wirkikai a cap with a befitting long red feather in it.

That would be a different matter for another occasion, another celebration.

That evening they would drink and take Ngong home to a wife who would be dissatisfied with the failure of the mission she had sent him out on but proud of the man to whom her parents had given her in marriage.

Bansos joyfully carried Ngong Wirkikai on their shoulders.

They had been such fools to doubt Ngong at any single moment. The great combatant had known what he was doing every minute of the ten the fight had lasted.

He had played the fool to let them make greater fools of themselves. He had lured the clever, overconfident, skilled Ibo boxer into a trap and then demolished him in style.

The Western was not necessarily better than the traditional after all. "Mati wun, mati wun, mati wun," was better than "Leave him alone, leave him alone, leave him alone."

Ngong Wirkikai had proven it with the "nkuum Nso".

Zow and the
Village Belle

INTRODUCTION

I was born and grew up outside my village in the different parts of the country to which my government worker of a father was transferred. We hardly went to the village and I can remember that I was about twelve when I was conscious of having gone to the place of origin of my parents for the first time.

I found my people in general and children of my age in particular quaintly primitive. I am sure I was the only child who wore shoes and clothes everybody considered sophisticated in my home area.

In those days, not only did adults of marriageable age also go to school, but a good number of them were actually married. They marvelled at the class I had attained in primary school at that tender age and marvelled even more at the fact that I would be going to secondary school the next year.

I felt positively different and everybody was kind to me and extremely flattered when I went visiting. They used to give me choice meals and make me eat until I could hardly breathe.

Yet, as I made my way home with a bloated stomach, villagers would call out to me from their thatched houses to come and eat or drink temptingly fresh nonalcoholic palm wine. I got to love the village and the people.

I had a lot of difficulties communicating with them in

the beginning since we did not speak our native language in my family at home. I remember my father asking people who questioned him about this abnormal situation in his house whether the native language was written in the General Certificate of Education.

In the village, immersion in the native language in every village activity made me grasp the essentials of the language fast. A few people who spoke broken English and others who had been to school helped out in the learning process.

I took special note of the togetherness of the villagers when a child was born and especially when someone died. No one went to work in the fields and the whole village assembled in the compound of the bereaved family for days on end. Music, food, drink and dance came out of every nook and cranny. The people were angelic.

My admiration for my village traditions and customs stayed with me for years after childhood and, as a young adult, I never missed any opportunity to return there and enjoy the company of those dear kind gentle folks. Unfortunately almost everything has changed but not my now anachronistic nostalgia.

The novella "Zow and the village belle" was born of that yearning for the good old ways. It is perhaps my lame effort to prove that I too belong and know and understand the ways of my people.

But for the names and the customs and traditions mentioned, the whole story came out of my imagination. A friend of a friend of mine borrowed the manuscript and read it. We did not know each other. Our first meeting nearly ended in a tragedy because a fight would have started right there in the street.

That morning a complete stranger blocked my way on the kerb in the Commercial Avenue in Bamenda. He glared at me and began to ask me questions. He was about the same height like me so he was able to look at me straight in the eye. I nearly shoved him out of my way to pass.

"Are you Mr. Kumengisa?" he asked.

I hesitated to answer for I thought he was being a trifle too bold to someone he had never met.

"Yes, I am," said I wryly, "and who would you be."

He put his arms akimbo and nodded mischievously several times.

"Never mind who I am," said the stranger, nodding some more. "You must be a very wicked man."

I was beginning to find it extremely difficult to bear the stranger's effrontery. I straightened to my full height.

"Look here," I said in annoyance bordering on anger, "I don't know who you are but – "

"Never mind who I am," the man went on. "Why did you kill that beautiful innocent young girl?"

My anger made me breathe faster.

"Just what are you talking about fellow?" I retorted. "I have never killed anyone in my life!"

The stranger's face lit up with a winning broad smile that wrinkled his temples and made his right mustache twitch.

"Couldn't you have made Anang marry her and let them live happily ever after?"

It is then that I understood. I took in a deep breath of relief. He must have read the manuscript of my novella "Zow"

"Oh dear!" I exclaimed. "Sir, I took you for serious and was beginning to lose my temper. I'm glad you liked the story."

"Liked the story?" he asked, thrusting his head forward. "Yes, until you killed the girl a second time. I would have punched you if you had been near me."

"Really?"

"How could you have made Anang suffer so much for nothing? I thought all would go well with Sei."

"I'm sorry I disappointed you so."

"You did worse than that. My wife read the story and wept."

"A pity."

He raised his right hand and pointed his forefinger in warning at me.

"Please, you must rewrite that story and give it a happy ending."

I churned the idea in my mind for a short while.

"Okay, Sir," I said finally, "I'll give it thought and see what I can make of it but – "

"No but about it," the angry stranger said forcefully. "Rewrite the story as a full novel and let the fruit tree bear fruit."

"I'll try."

"Do,: he said and winked with a friendly smile. "And write more stories."

"I surely will. Thanks a million."

"You're welcome."

He stepped out of my way, smiling some more, and with a bow, signalled me to move on.

For months after that I tried hard but failed to make "Zow" the novel he wanted. I am totally unable to give him satisfaction in that line but I am trying the other way.

RCK.

CHAPTER ONE

This story of great love and mysterious exchange is often told in my village. At the time the events in the story started, Zow M'bei was sixty-five years of age and considered very old indeed in the village despite the fact that she was as straight as a rod and walked without the assistance of a stick. People did not live long in those days.

Zow lived with her only child, a daughter by name Sei Kom Zow M'bei. Everybody thought Sei was Zow's child because of the resemblance between them notwithstanding the vast difference in age.

But Sei was really Zow's grandchild, daughter of her own only child Kom Zow M'bei who had died shortly after giving birth to Sei, her first child.

After the death of Kom, Zow was filled with loathing for the little witch who had taken the life of her beloved daughter. She glared at it with open hatred as it boxed the incorporate air with its clenched fists as if fighting back the ill feeling.

Zow thought all she needed to get even with the tiny thing was neglect. If she did not feed it, or fed it badly, it would presently follow Kom to the grave.

Its death would not raise any brows because infant mortality was very common. More infants died than survived.

Zow did not bat an eye the night after Kom's burial. She wondered why the god of her forefathers could have done her such a thing.

The hapless child too was terrible. It was a good timer. Each time she was about to fall asleep, it would start crying in an extraordinarily powerful voice.

Thus Zow tortured herself and was tortured by the infant until just before dawn when she fell into troubled sleep. This lasted only for a few minutes for she was woken by the women who had spent the night in her house.

They were up early to start cooking food for sympathizers who would begin arriving as soon as the sun showed its face above the horizon.

Zow got out of bed and checked the infant on the sheepskin beside her. It was sleeping peacefully. She did not have the heart to give it the intended killing hard look.

It was not the tiredness from lack of sleep that had influenced her. Something had happened to her that morning. Some bell in a part of her mind had begun a continuous ringing to remind her that the infant beside her was Kom's child, that it needed help and she could provide it if she would.

The sun was definitely rising under a different sky. Zow was her true self once more. When she took time to think over the matter, she was filled with shame.

The little thing was all she had in the world. Why should she destroy it? Its destruction would not even be revenge for it had not destroyed its own mother.

Its mother may only have been lost through it. A door is not responsible for the people who pass through it. Moreover, and above all, it was her beloved Kom's blood and therefore her own blood too.

Like herself, it had no one else in the world. Its father had died in a senseless hunting expedition four months before it was born. It and herself were two of a kind and should stick together. And the decision was obviously hers, Zow's, to take.

Zow was also an important person in the village. She thought of how she, a woman, had come to own a compound, a most uncommon situation in those days.

Her husband and his two brothers had all died in the same rainy season. He had gone first, then his two brothers had followed within a month.

Had the latter not died, one of them would have inherited her, taken the compound of two houses, and become a father to Kom who was then sixteen years old and had just been given away in marriage.

Both had been taken in witchcraft inside one week and, as their closest distant male relative did not want to hear of inheriting property with Zow as part of it, Zow had become the first and only female compound owner in the clan.

Word filtered to Zow that her husband's distant relative thought she was too correct for him. Her late husband, he was said to have said, was the only man in the whole clan to be suitable for her in everything.

Other men had been afraid to approach her for marriage although many confessed their attraction. Ownership of the compound may have been a deterrent. Who had ever heard of a woman owning a compound?

But there was more to it than just the compound. Zow had been dogged by ill luck all her life. Her only sister had not survived infancy. She herself had barely managed to get through after several attacks of the strong fever.

She had not really known her father because he had been taken away into slavery by white men with guns when she was not quite two years old.

Her mother had only lived long enough to give her to her husband. She now had no one she cared to be family with in the whole wide world.

If she did not give her love to Kom's child whom would she give it to? She should and would love Sei more than she had ever loved Kom.

The latter had after all played her a dirty trick by dying rudely before her. Mothers should die before their daughters.

Anyway, good sense demanded that she love Sei with all her heart. And she would. Kom's child might be the only good thing that ever happened to her. A good thing had to be given the chance to prove itself a good thing.

The most important secret society of women in the village found two nursing mothers for Sei. They would take turns at breast-feeding her until she attained the age of being weaned.

The feeding programme began at once and was carried out with the kindness that only countrywomen are capable of. Sei's breast mothers were regular and dedicated. Zow took care of everything else.

Zow had Sei weaned rather early, at sixteen months. Her good breast mothers should have a chance to attend to their own affairs.

The women of the secret society performed the rites of handing over and Zow took the child home and gave it all her love and most of her attention.

Time flies. So did Sei Kom Zow M'bei fly in growth. Soon she was a beautiful but rather delicate little girl.

Despite all the good food and love she had in abundance, she was ill most of the time. More was the part of her life she spent in illness than the one she spent in good health.

Herbalists and traditional doctors were in Zow's compound day in day out to take care of her. People began to fear that she might not make it into womanhood.

Zow too began to fear. Sei might play Kom's trick on her.

Mother and daughter would have used her in the same way. Her family would come to an end with her old self. She would rather die than see such a day.

Sei's continuous ill health, however, turned out to be what is called the "illness of growth". It made her grow fast. The work of the doctors was to keep her from pain and fevers until adulthood would take her out of the trouble.

Zow waited impatiently for the time to come. She would die of sheer anxiety and worry about her granddaughter. She was quite unable to relax and breathe well.

The day Sei would be a woman, she would start breathing fully once more. Sei continued in her remarkable growth. It seemed like an overnight thing.

Suddenly there was an oncoming young woman from nowhere. Once, on seeing her at play with her age mates, some sages of the village predicted that she would shake the whole clan when she became a woman.

Zow was secretly thrilled but playfully drove them away, saying they had "bad mouths". Young men passing near Zow's house often stopped to stare admiringly at Sei.

Zow pretended not to notice but her heart glowed with love, happiness and pride. Sei was growing out of childhood.

CHAPTER TWO

The day Sei turned fourteen, the village changed. It would never be the same again. A pearl had made its appearance within its precincts and the attention of its inhabitants was glued to it.

Young men went crazy. Every one of them fell for her. Each was determined to have her for wife. They ignored the fact that great beauty in the village went with a high bride-price.

Good things did not come easy and, as Sei was the best in the clan, she had to be necessarily the most difficult. Any man who did not see that was lucky since he would have little on his mind.

News about Sei spread quickly to neighbouring villages. Zow was bursting with pride. She had never loved Kom half as much as she loved her daughter.

Kom had been pretty but Sei was dazzling. She had not wasted her loving care. It had produced a lot more than she had expected.

She knew she did not have a long time to go. The last of her age mates had long been gone. She lived for only one thing now: giving her Sei away and giving her away the way she wanted before she would join her ancestors.

Sei would be married within two years and have a girl child in her first year of marriage. She would name the child and would then be free to take leave of the world with the satisfaction of achievement.

Suitors began to come in their numbers. It was not just anybody who came knocking. Zow was physically a big woman, taller than most men in the village and with shoulders that, in a man, would have been so good for carrying firewood from the bush.

She was also known to be as strong as a man and, although kind and reasonable, was possessed of a violent temper when provoked. Before coming to Zow's, a young man had to bear all this in mind.

Many of them, not sure of their eligibility, were afraid of being bodily thrown out by the big woman. This had never happened but everybody thought it a matter of time before it would.

Thus only the valiant ventured forth. Many came from far and wide and as many went back empty-handed.

Some came accompanied by their fathers, uncles, or elder brothers. Others alone, and others again timidly sent their friends or relatives, or both, to try on their behalf. Nobody succeeded.

The story was one of continuous failure but men did not stop coming and even coming again and again. Men love challenges. Here was a very great one indeed!

The road to Zow's house became the most used in the village. It was more used than the one to the palace. Yet its use was on the increase everyday.

Degrees of disappointment too kept increasing. A few young men had been known to leave Zow's house in tears. Most left more determined, clothed more in sadness than in anger.

Their sadness came from Sei's sympathetic look. It seemed to express her own disappointment at their failure. One young man fell out of Zow's house and rolled in despair on the ground, saying that the girl loved and wanted him but her mother and the villagers were against him.

The fear was that one of those good days a young man would be taken to the asylum in the chief's palace.

Zow was not rude to her visitors although their unannounced visits cost her a lot in hospitality. Sei bore the burden of cooking. Many said her meals were as tasty as she looked.

Zow was rigorous. What the suitors wanted was obvious. Only she herself knew what she wanted and it was out of place to tell any of them.

It was not wealth. It was not good looks either despite the tricky way she had of scrutinizing a young man's appearance without seeming to do so.

It was not good character she was after. A bull may as well have a good character. It would still be a bull and have a bull's head.

Too much cunning intelligence was out of question also. It could be used to trick and ridicule her innocent little girl.

What Zow wanted seemed complicated even to herself. She wanted a mixture. There would be character, appearance, intelligence, physical strength, wealth and a certain thing she could not put into words even in her mind. It had to do with Sei's safety, pride and comfort.

The correct man would have to be someone who would beat Sei if she pushed him to the wall and yet be able to go down on his knees in front of her when he wronged her.

He had to be one who would face a lion for her. She would be able to recognise such a man when he came. It was not going to take a long time, she was sure, before he would. The feeling ran strong in her blood.

The things that Zow thought and did were mixed up with the production from villagers' fertile minds. They said she wanted a lot of money because she was the owner of a compound.

She was the only person Sei had, so she would get both parts of the bride price: the mother's and the father's.

Male pride was touched to the quick but no man in the village, not even the chief, could talk mock in Zow's face and get away with it. Fate had worked matters out to favour her.

Here was a situation from which the lawmakers of the village would have made money, food and drinks. They gnashed their teeth and remained silent. If one avoided hunting vipers, one would live to the last day of one's lifespan.

Zow was grateful to the god of her ancestors to have more than compensated her for the loss of Kom who could never have generated such pleasurable disturbances from young men.

There had been some scramble for Kom's hand but that had been limited to their quarter of the village. She and her husband had enjoyed the attention it brought to their compound but he had died so shortly after Kom was taken.

Zow had been his only wife. He used to say she was big enough for several wives so he did not need to marry any others.

He had been good to her but she had lost him like every other good thing of hers. She hoped she would not lose Sei. She angrily banished the thought from her mind.

How could she invite ill luck to herself in such a foolish manner? Zow gloried in her granddaughter's appearance. She had become all woman in such a short time.

The lithe body, that graceful walk, the long neck above the sloping shoulders, the proud tenure of the head, those proud aggressive breasts and then the smooth face with lips of a darker brown, a comely nose and hypnotic light brown eyes were all features to make any man lose his head.

And about every marriageable man who knew her did.

46

People said she looked exactly like Zow had looked at the same age but Zow refused to listen to such foolish flattering talk. Who had been there to see her? She was probably the oldest person in the village.

She had always had too much of a man's build and physical strength to be truly beautiful. Her complexion had once been a light copper colour but age, hard work and exposure to the harsh tropical sun in the fields had made her almost raven black from a distance.

Closer she was a dark copper.

Sei was a shade darker than she had been at the same age but where her granddaughter had grace, she had had muscular agility. Sei was also a little shorter and much slimmer than she had been.

Outside the similarity in complexion, shape of the head and perhaps legs, there was little else she thought they had in common as far as looks went.

As for physical strength, Sei had only about half of what she had had at the same age. That would be enough to feed her husband and the children that would come.

Ah! What purpose did so much comparison serve anyway? The truth was that Sei was more woman than she had ever been. She was the most woman in the clan.

The more Sei blossomed, the more young men suffered. They sweated and worried their brains as they searched for a way to get the precious stone. They were surprised at her humility when they went courting.

She was always welcoming, available and seemingly willing. She stood midway between shyness and appreciable feminine boldness and was completely unaware of how beautiful she looked and the effect she had on men.

To her every young woman attracted the same number of

suitors as hers. It was the normal order and magnitude of events in a young woman's life before she got married.

She was not, however, in command of the situation. Parents guided their daughters towards the correct choice of a marriage partner. The only person she had was Zow. So everything depended on Zow. She was her parents.

If any man won Zow over to his side, Sei was his. Left to herself, Sei would have long been taken because of her kindness, inexperience and discomfort in the face of such fuss.

As it was, she had very little to say in the matter. Zow would guide her to the correct choice.

As the choice took a long time to come, some villagers began to look for something wrong in Sei. They wanted the grapes sour.

One day some young men ambushed her as she went to fetch water from the village brook. They began to tease her about her beauty. They accused her of showing it off by refusing men.

She told them that if she was beautiful at all, she had not done anything to acquire the beauty and should not be proud of it. As for a man, they knew that the choice was not hers to make.

If she had her way, she would have long chosen one of the many handsome young men who came to request her hand in marriage and been done with the whole thing.

She would already have had her own house and farms on which to grow crops.

The young men listened with mouths open. They had hoped for a rude answer to give them the opportunity of saying impolite things to her.

They were ashamed of their original intentions. She worsened matters by saying that each of them present was handsome enough for her to accept him as husband.

She looked at them straight in the eye as she said this. They all looked at their toes. Tradition had to be obeyed. She was right.

Sei's eyes did not shine with victory as she went back home with her gourd of water balanced precariously on her head. The young men looked at her with admiration for her body and her head.

With neither guile nor fear, she had defeated them. They enjoyed her defeat and loved her the more for being so wise at such a tender age.

CHAPTER THREE

One evening the chief's nephew arrived in the village from the coastal region of the country where he worked. He seemed to have come purposefully for Sei. The news took a short time to go round the village.

Everyone thought the right person had at last come. He had all that Zow required for the husband of her child. He had good looks in such quantities that he could have given away a whole calabashful and still have enough to be dashing.

Wealth was his. As for character, his had little to do with the rudeness of people who had been to school and looked down on both tradition and everyone else in the village.

When he greeted even the least important person in the village, he would give them his time and attention. Here was the correct match for Sei.

If Zow missed him, Sei would end up with a wastrel. And a good number of them was known to have come a-courting. More were definitely on their way.

The whole village was astir. The next day was going to be a day of days. It would be foolish to go to the farm and miss all the fun. Feasting would surely follow Sei's acceptance of the latest suitor.

Apart from being the chief's nephew, he was also the heir apparent to the throne royal of the village because our succession system is avuncularly matrilineal.

Everybody who was anybody in the village went to bed late that night. The chief's nephew had brought a jug of twenty litres of red wine to announce his arrival to the elders of the village.

He would be able to count on their moral and material support if he had come to do anything important in the village. The wine quickly went to people's heads and everyone declared that Anang—that was the name of the chief's nephew—was a man, a real man.

Wined that night or not, most villagers were up early the next morning. They were certain that they had predicted correctly.

Although during the party Anang had politely refused to react to their insinuations, dawn met him making his way in the company of his illustrious uncle, to Zow M'bei's compound.

Most of the village was watching. Curiosity in the country is unabashed. The chief was aware of all that was going on. Anang was not.

The duo entered the compound, went straight into Zow's house and sat down. It may have surprised Anang to find Zow already up and about. It was not for his sake. People get up early in the country to start doing their daily work.

They had hardly sat down when a crowd gathered at the door. Nothing similar had ever happened in the village.

Zow complained of its being rather early to wake the young lady they wanted to see. She usually woke her at sunrise but since the request was from "The Owner of the Village" himself, she did not have a choice.

She only hoped her little girl would not mind. Perhaps she was already awake as she was a light sleeper. Zow lit her brand new oil-lamp. The occasion warranted it.

Holding the lamp gingerly in her left hand, she crossed the room to behind the curtain where Sei lay on sheepskins on her bamboo bed.

She called her by name and was surprised when she did not answer. She called again, this time louder. No answer.

Then Zow shook her a little roughly by the shoulders. Sei's body went along stiffly with the action.

Zow stepped forward and peered into Sei's eyes. They were glassy and sightless.

She let go a horrible heart-rending scream which went far beyond the limits of the compound.

Sei was dead.

She had died in her sleep. Zow seemed about to drop dead. There was total confusion. The chief and his heir jumped out of their seats and sprang forward in unison to find out the truth for themselves.

Villagers rushed into the house and forced their way to the bedside to see and touch Sei to be sure she was really dead.

The news slapped the village in the face. By now the sun's face was fully above the horizon. In a short time the whole clan had heard the horrid news. Most people refused to believe it and came from far to see for themselves. Could beauty of such greatness perish so easily?

The time they had expected Sei to die had long passed. A good tree grows into maturity to bear fruit, not to die. There is something wrong with a tree that either dies at maturity or thereafter does not bear fruit to let people taste of its being.

Some elders thought the death served Zow right. She had made her daughter too precious and the real owner had decided to take her back. She had refused giving her daughter to anyone. Look what had happened.

A good number of elders went to Zow's compound to take pleasure in her pain. They would see her as the common, ordinary woman she was and not the strong one they feared to talk to about her abnormal position of female man in the community.

Zow was inconsolable in her grief. When villagers genuinely sympathized with her, she barked at them as if they were mocking at her.

She at last sat on her bed with her cheeks held between her palms. She did not look beaten. Only furious, wild and determined. Not a tear was in her eye. She was indifferent to the wailing of those around her.

Young men rolled on the ground and shamelessly cried along with the women. Anang wept passionately.

The chief could take no more and fled to his palace for fear that he would be seen weeping. There had been shocking deaths in the village before but none had ever hit so hard, or so far.

It was worse than when lightening had struck and killed ten people from various families four years back.

Zow's compound was packed full. People sat on the ground. Some sat on bamboo benches in front of the empty house opposite Zow's. Others on stones they had picked up from behind the houses.

The rest just stood around watching. Everybody felt the great impact of the loss. The sight that embellished people's morning as they went to the farm was gone forever.

~ ~ ~

Stranger happenings were in store for the village. Zow was to be the centre of them all. There had been a spell of reprieve in the mourning when some kind of madness took hold of her.

She sprang from her bed like a young girl and shot out of the house like an arrow. People dived out of her way and everybody held their breath, spellbound. The smell of deep fear was everywhere. Whom did Zow suspect of having killed her child by use of witchcraft?

This type of death was the work of nothing else but witchcraft. In anger would Zow not pounce on just anybody?

And with that size, that strength, that rage, would she not be able to knock down even the strongest of men not to mention women?

Zow was away for a few minutes. Everyone was afraid to look in the direction in which she had gone, to find out what she was up to. She might suddenly appear and lock eyes with an unfortunate person. The person would be in for it.

At last they heard her coming back. In her right hand was a long guava sapling the thickness of a man's thumb. They all knew the toughness of the guava.

Villagers scattered like ants in front of her as she strode towards her door, brandishing the guava. She swung into the house and made straight for her granddaughter's bedside.

The suspense was so great that people seemed to stop breathing.

Zow's naked shrivelled bosom rose and fell in rhythm with her breathing as she stood glaring down at her grandchild. She was breathing through the mouth.

Her eyes emitted fire that would have made holes in a dry leaf. She stood there for several minutes. The house was still in dead silence.

All attention was on the tall woman looking down at the dead body of the beautiful girl on a bamboo bed.

Zow tore off the curtain in front of the bed in a violent movement. Villagers closest to the bed jumped back.

Everybody was afraid. No one dared utter the least word or make any unnecessary movement. And most of them were men.

Sei's body was exposed in better light. Her loin cloth had

loosened and slipped down almost to her navel. Her belly was flat in her slim body.

Her breasts pointed proudly up to the ceiling of brown mats. Her eyes were lightly closed on the calm face. There was the trace of a smile in the corners of her soft mouth. She was lovely even in death.

Women clapped their hands at the great loss. Some men bowed their heads in shame at what was going on in their minds. A few of these struggled to hide the reaction in their bodies.

The rest were sad and pensive. Such beauty should have stayed alive to belong to some worthy man. Death had turned out to be the greater suitor and winner. It was enjoying everything.

Zow pushed everyone out of their dreams into reality. She took a menacing step forward with the guava in her hand. Her eyes were fixed on her granddaughter.

Greater silence took hold of the house now. It echoed through the compound to the limits of the village. Zow deepened it even more as she stood there thrust forward with the guava sapling in her hand pointing at the earthen floor.

The sapling rose and would have come down on Sei, for that was Zow's intention, had a young man, the width of two fingers held together taller than Zow, not stepped out of the half circle around Sei's bed and gently but firmly taken hold of the guava in mid-air.

It was Anang the chief's nephew.

Without looking round Zow knew who it was. With the corner of her eye she saw her whip make its way from hand to hand towards the door until it disappeared in the lake of villagers in the yard.

Zow's eyes were still glued to Sei's body. Her bosom still

rose and fell as she continued to breathe through her mouth. She let escape a little laugh without mirth through her hardened lips. Then she began to nod her head like a lizard, in physical affirmation of something that was going on in her mind.

"Good, young man," she said through gnashed teeth, putting her strong arms akimbo. "Save her fine looks. Perhaps they'll be yours some day for some time. *Asia*. It'll be borrowed time."

She did not sound angry. She only seemed profoundly dissatisfied.

There appeared a cunning look in her eyes as she bent over her granddaughter. The people were perplexed. What could the old woman possibly be up to? They were not to worry for long.

Zow began to slap Sei on the cheeks. At first it was a slow rhythmic action. The slaps were not the vicious ones of anger but those a mother would give a child for correction.

Zow's speed of delivery increased quickly. When it suddenly became very fast, the people in the house cried out. Dismay gripped the whole compound.

The crowd was beginning to move about restlessly. They were wondering what to do with Zow in her disturbed state of mind when reactions from Sei's body caught their attention.

The progression was interesting. At first Sei's head was moved by the force of the blows from her grandmother. Then it began to move on its own, trying to dodge from the blows. The eyes were still calmly closed.

The movements became more obvious and violent. Then the eyes opened, the brows drew together in a frown and Sei raised her arms to her face in defence.

"No Zow, don't!"

It was Sei's voice. It came out like a brook flowing over pebbles.

"It's alright," replied Zow. "All's fine now."

More than half the crowd simply vanished from the compound although there was nothing really frightening about the half naked body of the most beautiful young woman in the clan, lying dazed on her bed.

Anang stepped forward, took Sei by the shoulders and helped her into a sitting position. He stood looking at her, absorbing all he had not had the chance to see and admire before.

The sun peeped in through the tiny opening that served as window in the back wall of the house. Anang was moved. Sei drew up her loin cloth over her breasts and looked round at the overcrowded and stuffy house.

Her eyes hesitated for a brief second on the stranger who had held her. She had never seen him in her life. She wondered why she had let a complete stranger hold her.

It had all happened unexpectedly. The rumours about him and his intentions had reached her, of course. He looked frightfully handsome but there was nothing
disturbing in his simple, humble reassuring countenance.

Zow watched in silence. She was satisfied.

"Young man," she said, "you are fit for her. You've got the strength. But the future may not be good for you. What she now has is borrowed. I wish it were not. I've only done my best. You'll know more tomorrow."

"Thank you mother," Anang answered with his head bowed. His mind was more on respect than on the meaning of Zow's words.

Zow sat down on Sei's bed. She looked at her granddaughter and her granddaughter looked at her. Then they held hands like lovers and sat like that for a long time.

Villagers were timidly filling up Zow's house again. They

watched Zow and daughter in silence. Sei would not ask the question everyone expected her to ask. When her grandmother would be ready, she would tell her all she wanted to know.

"Mother!" cried Anang of a sudden. "What kind of people are we? Have we forgotten our tradition? This kind of thing has never happened in the land. It calls for celebration. The God of our ancestors is with us. Let us thank Him."

Those words put everybody into action in the whole village. The most unexpected of deaths had never taken the villagers by such surprise.

This had reached the worst of sudden deaths and come back to be more than a birth. It was a resurrection, a much higher thing than birth and death put together.

Sei thought she liked a man who was conscious of his tradition. She avoided thinking that she liked Anang. She wondered what it took to go to school.

She would love to go to school for a few years. Anang must know so many things. She would see.

CHAPTER FOUR

A mighty feast would take over the day. Nearly all villagers disappeared from Zow's compound to prepare for it. Only a few slow old women were left in the yard when Zow let go of Sei's hand. Her face bore the look of a warrior who had won the decisive battle in a war.

"My beloved little one," she said to her Sei, folding her arms over her flat old bosom. "I could not let it happen to me again. Your mother successfully did it. At that time I was much younger and had a lot less knowledge of the world. Today, I am wiser with age. I refuse to let you treat me the same way your mother did."

In her gentle way, Sei turned to face Zow.

"Zow, what is it that I have done without knowing?" she asked. "Please, mother tell me. I can make amends."

"Did you not see the whole village here in our compound?" Zow replied.

Sei swung her long legs over Zow's head and brought them down on the floor. Because of the love between her and Zow, Sei could get away with breaking a few minor traditional rules of behaviour.

"Of course, I did," Sei went on light-heartedly. "What were they here for? Tell me what it was you stopped me from doing?"

The sounds of drums were already coming from the direction of the palace. "You died child," Zow answered, "but I did not let you stay dead. I beat you

out of it."

Sei sat straighter on the bed.

"Zow, what are you talking about?" she asked.

Her eyes had become big and round.

"You died child," said Zow calmly. "You went your way to join your mother and leave me here, old and alone."

A dreamy look replaced the surprise on Sei's face.

"Was that dying?" she asked. "I was in a distant fine country with green hills, beautiful orchards and clear water streams in the valleys. It was wonderful."

"I'm sure it was," agreed Zow. "To you, there. Not to me here. Your mother went thither but left me you. Whom did you leave me? You think I came here to stay forever? I must go before you now, to join my mother, yours and my husband."

"Why do you talk about death like that Zow?"

"Don't interrupt me child!" cried Zow. "There's no time. When I go you'll mourn for a year as required. Then you can marry the chief's nephew if it'll be possible. I wholeheartedly approve of him but—"

"Abba Zow," exclaimed Sei. "You talk as if death is a thing you've planned."

"Well, perhaps I have, perhaps I haven't," said Zow calmly. "Do you think birth and death are pure accident? It is the Father of the World who knows exact times and places. If we know how to get in touch with him he may show us one or two things to help us."

"Zow you really sound so strange, so mysterious today."

"You too have been more than that today child." A touch of exhaustion crept into Zow's voice. "Come let's join in the feasting. They are celebrating your death, you know? It would be morning again before they are done."

Sei hesitated. She would have liked them to continue the conversation but musicians from the palace had invaded the compound. Behind them came a crowd loaded with food and drink. Everybody was dancing happily and energetically.

Train after train of people entered Zow's compound, carrying food and drink. Food came from every kitchen and palm wine from every palm bush in the village.

The feast had begun, and as it was Sei's, she had to be fully involved in it. Zow gave her the support she needed.

Anang brought two bottles of whisky, two jugs of twenty litres of red wine and several crates of beer. The villagers had never seen so much white man drink at one time.

It was enough for every man to have a meaningful sip and there would still be a little left for the important women of the village.

The chief sent a big goat that was slaughtered in the compound. When it would be cooked, he would be invited from the palace to officially open the strange death celebration of a living person.

At the correct moment, the chief came from the palace and set the ball rolling and how the people did feast! There had never been such a function in the village.

Zow took a little red wine in her aluminium mug and shared it with Sei. It was all she would let them drink but they tasted of every dish that was brought in accordance with the tradition of the village. Sei was bursting at the seams.

While people ate and drank, dancing groups came into the centre of the compound in turns to show their new styles and revive the old ones.

Anang showed himself a great dancer in a number of the groups and Zow nodded her head in admiration. Sei looked at the ground between her feet. Watchful villagers pretended not to have noticed.

Then it was time for "Ndong", the dance for all. Everybody was on their feet. Even the chief himself got up and took a few dignified steps round the compound. Men shouted praises at him. Women ululated. The villagers were proud to have such a lively chief.

When the chief had done, Zow stepped out a little towards the centre of the compound. She danced on the spot and, amidst more ululation from the women, Sei danced shyly behind her grandmother.

At midnight Anang escorted the chief to the palace, lighting the way with his powerful electric torch. A number of villagers followed in their wake. At second cock's crow the remaining villagers thought enough was enough and, having lit torches made from bamboos, left in groups.

Everybody was tired and saturated right to their bone marrow with drink and food.

Zow and Sei went to bed immediately after the last villager left. They fell asleep even before they had finished pulling their blankets over their shoulders. With the tiredness they slept very deeply so that it turned out to be an even shorter night.

Sei was the first to get up and went to fetch water from the brook. When she came back she put some semblance of order into the great disorder which reigned in their compound.

She warmed some of yesterday's food for breakfast and went to wake her grandmother. Sei opened the little traditional window on the wall behind Zow's bed.

Light flooded Zow's bed but did not disturb her. Sei thought it strange. She pulled the blanket away from her grandmother's shoulders playfully in little jerks. Zow was stiff.

She took an apprehensive look at her face and caught her breath. She looked closer. Zow's eyes stared fixedly at the wall in front of them. Sei tried in vain to turn her grandmother round to face her.

Zow was as stiff as a log of wood. She was not breathing. Though Sei had no experience at all with death, she realised that her Zow was dead. She had to be.

Sei let out a scream that ran through the neighbouring compounds like a long drawn out echo. When the first neighbours arrived, she had fainted. They poured cold water on her to bring her back to consciousness.

While most of them were waiting anxiously for Sei to come to, the rest turned to Zow. She was truly dead.

The shock again went through the whole village. Zow's compound once more became the place of assembly. Were Zow and her daughter using death as a toy?

Women of Zow's secret society immediately took her body away to prepare it for burial in their special way. They would hand it over to the men when they would be through. The latter would inter it.

Sei wept out her very soul. Her grandmother had deliberately died, she said. She had talked about death in a knowing way the night before. She had even given her instructions on how long she was to stay after her death before getting married.

Sei felt that her world had come to an end. She would have to stay for a whole year before getting married. Where would she stay during that time?

Why had Zow not given her away in marriage before dying? What would she tell Kom was the last thing she had done here on earth? What was she, a mere child, expected to do during the funeral of her grandmother?

A lot of Sei's questions were answered for her. She was to stay with the elder, who was also the fatter, of the women who had breast-fed her as an infant.

It would be in her house that Anang would come to fetch her for marriage. The palace would take care of everything that had to do with Zow's burial.

The latter was already considered a mother-in-law and Anang, of course, her husband, but for certain rights to be performed in about a year. Zow had not given them the opportunity to perform the betrothal ceremony. It could no longer be done since she was not.

After Zow was buried, in front of her house, the women of her secret society stayed the whole week of eight days with Sei. They tried to be many Zows to her.

On the ninth day, her new mother took her to her house in her husband's vast compound of ten wives, each in her own house.

There, to forget her great loss, Sei buried her head in farm work. When Anang was leaving back for the coast, she did not spend as much time with him as he had hoped. But he understood.

Sei had gone back to the good hands she had started life in. She was better taken care of than most young women in the clan but Zow was on her mind all the time.

The hard work she immersed herself in did not take away the permanent picture of her grandmother from her side. Once in a while, her foster mother would catch her talking seemingly alone. The mention of the name of Zow would tell who her companion was.

Witchdoctors were finally summoned to drive Zow away. Sei was surprised. If the whole thing was not all in her mind and Zow was often with her, what was wrong with that? Was that not some kind of protection or even guidance?

Somehow the doctors succeeded and she was never again found talking to Zow or any other spirit.

CHAPTER FIVE

The year was a very short one for Sei. She had time for nothing but work in the farm, coming back home late and going to bed early only to be up early the next day and head back for the farm.

Villagers talked a great deal about her. Her husband and children would know no want as she would produce a lot more food than they would need. She herself felt she would be happy with Anang but a little voice kept disturbing her inside.

The problem was not Anang. It was whether the final rites of the marriage would ever be performed. Zow had said certain things that she did not understand but would not discuss them with anyone.

Zow's compound had been taken by a distant relative of her grandfather, the one, she was told, who had refused inheriting the compound many years before if Zow was going to be a part of it.

A part of her would always be there in that compound even if Zow had not been buried there. The way to one of her farms was close to it and she often felt something close to a physical pull whenever she passed by it.

That was where Zow's death celebration was going to take place. As it was going to be a palace affair, it would certainly be grand. Anang would have a very important part to play in it.

Since shortly after the occasion he would have to come

back to the village for his marriage, the chief had thought it best for the two events to be exceptionally done together, or one closely followed by the other.

Anang would thus avoid having to ask for permission two times at short intervals from his boss, the white man.

Sei's people agreed to the idea without the usual hesitation from in-laws. She had once thought she had no family. It took Zow's death for her sisters, brothers—we do not have cousins in our language—aunts and uncles to appear from every nook and cranny in the village.

During Zow's death celebration and her marriage, even more would surface. They would provide food and be fed, support and be supported. No one had ever been heard to lack family in the village.

Two days before Zow's death celebration was to start, the chief and his family began to worry because Anang had not arrived. That very afternoon the heir apparent arrived and arrived in grand style. A long train of carriers from the big town some ten miles away carried his luggage. There were ten strong men.

In what they carried were drinks for the two events. White men's drinks did not get spoilt in the bottles until these were opened. It was possible to keep them for years on condition that they were not opened. So there was no fear for them. They would be as good as new when they were wanted.

The carriers also brought in presents for everybody, even those only remotely related to Anang's in-laws, the palace or his parents. These were in two voluminous trunks which had squeezed a great deal of sweat out of those who had carried them.

The things were all packed in the palm wine stores in the palace. Anang paid off the carriers and turned to formally greet his uncle. Everybody was relieved and happy.

The chief apprised Anang of his decision. Anang welcomed it. They both spent the next day doing what had not been done and putting finishing touches to what had been done. They took their time as these were going to be the greatest of events the village had ever taken part in.

They first bore in mind the satisfaction of Anang's in-laws, his own family and then the villagers and any visitors from the rest of the clan. Anang managed to go to bed early that evening so as to be up early the next morning, to be up to the great tasks ahead of him.

He was anxious but tradition did not permit him to show eagerness to see Sei. She had certainly heard of his arrival. It would be bad taste for her to ask for or about him.

Anang had to finish with the important part of the preparation first. A bombshell fell on goats in the palace in the small hours of that important morning. In all fifteen goats were killed.

Two mighty boars and a young bull officially joined the goats. Two basins full of chicken heads in the centre of the courtyard showed how many chickens had been killed.

Half of the meat and half of the huge quantity of raw food in the courtyard were taken to Zow's compound for the death celebration while the other halves were left in the palace for the next day, the day of the marriage ceremony and banquet.

Anang divided the drinks he had brought in the same way. His uncle would take care of the details. Palm wine would be like the water that flowed unceasingly in the brook the village drank from.

It would be rude to be meticulous in sharing it in a palace death celebration, not to mention a palace marriage feast. He would feel really free when the two burdens were off his shoulders.

He turned to the gifts he had brought. He sent Sei the suitcase of clothes he had specially selected for her. The next day the women in her family would decide what she would put on at different moments of the day, the most important day in their lives.

Gifts in the two trunks were labelled with pieces of paper on which names were written. A little prince in the final year of primary school read out the names of the owners. The gifts were either taken by the owners themselves or members of their family.

The distribution took some time but it was necessary because most of the clothes were going to be put on for the death celebration.

From the bottom of his heart, Anang thanked all those who had assisted in the slaughtering of the animals and preparing things for the feast.

When he said everybody was to go home and get dressed for the party, spontaneous applause broke out and he slipped from the courtyard.

Dancing in honour of Zow's memory began before sunrise. *Mbaya* went round the village with a hot number to get slow people out of their beds.

The dancers settled round the old woman's grave with a calabash of palm wine to clear their throats as villagers began to arrive with their contributions of drink and cooked food.

Every dance group in the village warmed the compound to await the real thing when the chief arrived. Each group was given breakfast and a big calabash of palm wine. By the time the chief arrived everybody was warm and ready.

The chief came in great pomp and poured the customary libation. The traditional cock was brought. He cut its head off, and then its right wing and threw these on Zow's grave. That was her share.

He then served his nobles in their cups and then the family-in-law in their cupped hands. He danced for a short time with one of the groups of dancers to set the ball rolling, then sat amongst his nobles in front of Zow's house.

The applause that came from the happy villagers was deafening.

Dancers in their various groups were showing off their latest styles and being rewarded with coins, kola nuts, cupfuls of drink or roasted meat. The dancing made the blood boil in the young and brought the old back to middle age.

Those who had "four eyes" said Zow was happy, very happy. But only on one side of her face. So they said.

Anang and his friends nearly danced themselves lame. They were all over the place, rewarding here, showing off a new style there, calling remarks across the compound to let people know that this was the death celebration of an in-law with a difference.

When Anang danced in front of Sei's foster mother, a big white cock appeared in her hands and she wiped the sweat from his clean-shaven face with its body. The cock was taken away to be specially kept for him. The people shouted and applauded.

Then the men's dance groups started firing guns in turns. The compound was dark with smoke into which twilight merged but the people were happy and danced on and on.

Sei and her friends had little breathing space. They had to serve so many people repeatedly. The villagers ate and ate and ate but the food would not get finished. Then they drank and drank and got drunk but the drinks would not get finished.

The men were strong. They danced and sweated off their drinks and drunkenness and started drinking again and dancing even more. Whenever the level of food or drink became low in their stomachs, they went for more.

Time came for young women to dance. Sei was thrilled to dance with her age mates who took away for safe keeping the gifts Anang and his friends heaped on her. Several hurricane-lamps were brought from the palace and neighbouring compounds to light up the celebration grounds.

Midnight came and passed. The women danced on. To Sei's relief they at last stopped for a long drink but began dancing again. Some of them flitted around the compound as if they had not danced for such a long time before.

Sei marvelled. By first cock's crow Sei was so tired that she could barely drag her heavy legs about.

The big fire in the centre of the compound was beginning to lose its heat and brightness and she sat on a stone facing where Zow lay in her grave. The big fire grew weaker and weaker.

She must have dozed off because she woke with a start. When her friends who, unknown to her had been watching from a distance, asked what the matter was, she said her grandmother had appeared above her grave and was beckoning to her. Could they not see Zow sitting on a golden chair on her grave?

Her friends thought she was exhausted and guided her from the yard to Zow's house. They led her to her famous bed, the one on which Zow had beaten her back from the dead.

They put her to bed like a baby but did not bother to find something to cover her with as the inside of the house was fairly warm.

Sei immediately fell asleep and her friends looked for Anang and told him not to disturb her rest since he would disturb it totally the next night.

Anang laughed and went to give a hand in kindling of the big fire. His friends were piling wood over the burning splinters. He was happy with them. He would be able to count on their moral support at sunrise, when he would be required to display his best styles with his bride by his side.

The fire was going well again when he thought he saw his late grandmother-in-law walk briskly past and enter the house where his bride lay.

He stepped over an old witch doctor gnawing toothlessly at a chicken leg and followed uncertainly what he thought he had seen.

When he entered the house, there were only tired women sleeping as best they could on the floor of the overcrowded house. Two bright hurricane-lamps, hung from the ceiling in the centre of the large room, made it easy for him to see his way towards the right corner where he had witnessed the miracle of Sei's resurrection.

He was relieved to find Sei in bed. She moved slightly and he went over to her. He was not afraid because he was not out for any wrongdoing. He sat down at the edge of the bed.

Sei turned and looked into his face in the half light. Her face was grave. She took his hand and held it in her soft one. His heart was at first full of love and tenderness but suddenly it turned to stone.

Sei seemed to have something unpleasant to tell him. As he moved closer to her, fat tears rolled down her beautiful cheeks.

He fought the urge to take her into his arms.

"What is it Sei?" he asked in alarm.

Sei sobbed silently for a minute, washing his hand with her hot tears.

"My dear husband Anang," she said in a strange strained voice. "Zow has come."

Anang sprang up and rushed out of the house. That had been the best witchdoctor in the village by the fire.

He rushed out over the bodies of the sleeping women and

took the old man by the arm. He did not have time to explain. The old man understood. They hobbled into

Zow's house. Sei still lay as he had left her. He flashed his torch on her chest. It was still. She was not breathing.

She was dead.

THE BRIEF STOP

THE BRIEF STOP

The thirty-sitter Toyota bus took a sharp bend and suddenly encountered a mighty silent crowd in the middle of the road. People were staring into a makeshift playground some ten yards wide in front of them.

They were all open-mouthed with shock and none of them was paying the least attention to the danger of the moving automobile on the dry laterite track.

The driver slammed on the brake pedal and the bus came to an abrupt screeching and skidding stop with passengers lurching angrily forward.

A furious woman in black started to say something, shut her mouth for a spell and opened it again in unison with the rest of the passengers as they beheld a sight of unimaginable horror.

They all spilled out of the bus and mingled pell-mell with the stunned population which had inadvertently interrupted their journey.

Three bulky women elbowed their way to where they could have a good look at the bloody spectacle. They began screaming, one after the other and then very loudly together, uniting their throaty emissions with leg action that was a clumsy imitation of a dash, towards the safe haven of the interior of the bus.

In the middle of the place for play the headless body of a seven-year-old boy was dancing on the spot with blood spouting rhythmically from its neck onto the sparse brownish dry season grass around.

The head lay a yard from it with the tongue hanging grotesquely out of the mouth and the unblinking eyes looking sightlessly at the bus. The woman in black rushed across the road and began throwing up on the dusty roadside.

"God!" an effeminate male voice exclaimed tearfully from within the crowd. "He knocked the innocent thing unconscious and sliced off its head like that of a common goat."

The passengers were silent but unable to look elsewhere. Everybody was looking intently at the shaking human remains on the ground. Twice did a dull velvety sweeping sound come from them.

Standing some three yards from the body, in a dirty yellow shirt, a young man of about nineteen was watching the violent movements of the body indifferently.

A drowsy sardonic smile twisted his parched blackened lips and he swayed unsteadily back and forth as if in drunken stupor. In his right hand he held a razor-sharp, brand new cutlass dripping with blood.

Under his scrutiny the convulsions of death throes suddenly stopped and the little body lay still. The multitude came alive. In pent up fury it emerged from the inactivity of its confused warm late afternoon trauma and everybody began to talk and gesticulate at the same time.

The killer brandished his cutting edge and stepped forward. People stopped talking and jumped out of his way. More murder shone in his lethargic eyes as more and more of the crowd cleared the way for him. One man stood his grounds.

It was a tall slim clean-shaven Aku man of the colour of copper, wearing a long white robe over cream baggy trousers. He stood squarely in the way of the man of blood who raised his weapon to shoulder level as he advanced.

Most of the people cried out. The killer quickened his pace and looked fiercely up into the cowhand's face. The latter was not impressed. He did not budge but watched his opponent's movements closely.

He suddenly narrowed his eyes and began to twirl his stick round his head. The killer raised his cutlass. In a flash the view of the stick was lost in the cattle hand's faster and faster movement.

Then came the sound of the impact of wood against flesh and bone. The cutlass went flying harmlessly over the decapitated body and landed on grass.

The killer hollered, bent his head left and let his right hand hang uselessly at his side. People had hurriedly been gathering stones and sticks for an obvious reason and sprang forward, stemming any further action from the stick-wielding Muslim.

They fell on the teenage scoundrel like bees. They hit him with anything they could lay hands on and on any part of the body nearest them.

He tried to fight back but they were too many for him and he was soon overpowered and crashed to the ground. Now began slow meticulous beating with sticks, pelting with stones, boxing and random kicking.

When he seemed to have lost consciousness, the irate mass stopped to watch him die. Then he made a fatal mistake – he tried to rise from his position. A myriad blows thrust him back.

New action came from behind. A heavy-breathing giant of a man, grunting in action, with a stone four times the size of his large head in his arms, pushed his way through the mob and stood astride the teenager's upturned gory forehead.

Someone cried out "Noooo!". The huge man raised the stone. It seemed to suspend there in mid-air for a long second and then came down onto the target with great force, accompanied by the most nerve-racking of muted sounds. The head became an ugly, partly hairy, red and off-white pancake.

Blood and brains, hair and crushed skull splashed on the feet of the onlookers nearest to the smashed head. In the ensuing stampede, people stepped on the horrid mixture underfoot.

Muscles on the half-exposed chest twitched. Finally the legs straightened and the body shuddered and lay still. In various ways people expressed their surprise. They wanted to know what the world was coming to and began to disperse rather guiltily.

The bus driver blew his horn. In silence passengers quickly took their places in the bus once more. The road was now fairly clear. They drove into it. The siren of an ambulance reached them from somewhere behind.

They moved on, bearing in mind remorsefully how that was the longest road brief stop they had ever had. They avoided looking at their shoes and wished it had all been a nightmare. The bus kept picking up speed. It was no dream.

THE WARDER'S ASSIGNMENT

INTRODUCTION

"The Warder's Assignment" is the forerunner of a novel entitled "The Legacy" and a full story in its own right. An old warder provides the writing materials for a novel to a man on death row.

Before the condemned man is killed, he has developed a close relationship with the warder and given him the manuscript in two big exercise books with detailed instructions on how the book was to be published.

The warder takes his assignment very seriously indeed and has his own contribution to make in the story of the event that shook all Ubea and ended with the author being sentenced to death for double murder.

Before handing the manuscript over to the publisher, the warder treats the latter of a painful ailment got from too much enjoyment of the good life the night before, tells him his philosophy of life and what he thinks happened that resulted in the writing of the book he wants printed.

He sits in the printer's office and makes him write down verbatim all that he has to say. The printer's hands are tied in more than one way and he discovers that he must do as the warder says. He goes through the ordeal and is relieved when the old warder finally has his say and leaves. He takes his time to read the difficult manuscript partly in the office and partly at home.

The next day he meets the sponsor of the work, mother of the executed author and they do not only plan out together how the work is to be done, but he gets paid for the work in advance and decides he would publish "The Warder's Assignment" to prepare the grounds for the coming of "The Legacy".

Here now is "The Warder's Assignment", "The Legacy" is on its way.

RCK

CHAPTER ONE

The saying goes that when trouble sleeps pride wakes it up for action. People are always in action, looking for ways to wake sleeping trouble to act. When it is fully in action, they have the opportunity to prove that they are tough. Thus the saying "when the going gets tough, the tough get going" sounds so correct.

Men are more anxious to prove this true with their action than women. So when the going gets tough, they think they are tough when they too get going, whatever their definition of toughness is.

I was to discover that, like most men, when the going got tough, I did not get going. I stayed put, and knew it. That was humiliating.

Most men think that a major way of getting tough is holding one's alcohol once it has been consumed. The more one can withstand its effects, the tougher one claims to be, thinks one is, or is said to be by those of the drinking world.

That is pride peculiar to men who drink and it is my belief that more men drink than not and most often drink with the intention of achieving intoxication which they want to vanquish in the name of toughness.

How much of that poison – for that is what alcohol is – can a man take before he gets to his ambition of losing his mind?

The unfortunate thing is that the quantity, depending on

the power and the type of drink, varies from man to man and, in the same man, from day to day.

I have brought up this point before the story I am going to tell because, without the drinking extravaganza I got involved in, I might not have got drunk – no, "drunk" is not the word for no real drinker ever admits to ever getting drunk – I may not have been sick from drinking too much and may not have met my story.

I would not have sought to run away from domestic trouble by going to the office earlier than usual and may not have met the man who gave me the story to which this one is an introduction.

Chain reaction from one incident of drinking led me onto what I will write on the following pages before undertaking to present what I have edited which came from a young man who passed on a couple of years ago.

I am saying that from drinking, one thing led onto the other until I got to   printing the biography, if I may call it that, of a person people called "a convicted felon" – whatever that means.

My foresight turned out to be correct for, after reading the book, most of these same citizens changed their minds about the felon and went further to question the system of meting out justice we inherited from our colonial masters, we now being, of course, an independent and kind of self-governing nation. Again,   whatever all that means.

I remember everything as if it was yesterday. I mean everything concerning the work I was called upon to do on the book. I only hazily retain a few things about the trial which was the deciding event in the book.

I had not gone to court because I travelled to Nigeria to buy machinery, paper and ink for the little printing press that I had just started.

It had taken me many years to plan out and save for that business. I was not about to give it up because of a case that had come out of the blues. The case was a hot cake but my business was hotter.

The information I had about the case came from my wife and heated discussions and debates in public houses in town. For once my spouse made history by showing interest and partaking in a public issue that did not concern the Baptist Church or religion as a whole.

She described in great detail how the court had been packed full during the days of the trial.

There had followed four months of waiting to give the judge time to come out with a judgment. It all depended on one person since our judicial system is monolithically individualistic and so has nothing in common with a jury.

The verdict was execution by hanging.

It surprised me because I had hoped that the fellow would be given something less. Perhaps "life". I did not want to give the matter heavy thought. Moreover I had too much on my mind to spare time unduly for it. It would not change anything.

My wife got me out of my detachment by bringing up the matter for discussion one Saturday morning during breakfast.

I gave her only part of my attention as I wrote out plans for my work for the day.

She intermittently glared at me for my inattention. I would catch sight of her with the corner of my eye as she swelled dangerously in her light blue nightdress.

I did not want her to explode so, at last, I decided to hear her out. I stopped work completely and put my pen down ceremoniously on the table.

She started with how she felt. She did not like the lawyer the state had given the defendant. She used the word! She had made a lot of progress in jurisprudence.

She wanted to know how the state, in a matter of the state versus the young man, could have chosen a lawyer for him, the accused?

She did not like the poor language of the judge. He was also a stuffed shirt who paid much more attention to the appellation of "my lord" and the trappings of his position than to the solemn matter in hand.

What she hated most was the betrayal of the best friend of the accused. My wife had come back home with a handbag full of new vocabulary in legal terminology.

I waited for her to tell me what the betrayal of the best friend had consisted in. I knew what she wanted but would not play the game. She waited for me to ask her. I did not.

I picked up my pen casually and started writing again. She lost her temper. She accused me of indifference and lack of interest in her. She said that I was always like that.

I pleaded with her to continue the story with my pen poised in the air. She would not. Her narration ended there. She cleared the table of the cups and other breakfast things with unwarranted energy.

I tried to tell her that it did not matter anymore since the young man had been hanged and subsequently buried. She asked me whether I would be counted if they were counting human beings in the world.

I answered in the negative calmly, wondering why she had married me if I was an animal. She sighed deeply as they do in Nigerian films and wagged her narrow waist as she swung empty-handed into the kitchen before coming back for the tray of teacups she had forgotten to take.

I had glanced at the opinions of various journalists in the newspapers in town but had so many other eggs to fry that I soon let the whole thing drop.

I did not know that in a few weeks the whole cake would be brought to me on a platter of gold in my office by a person that I would never have connected with books, and in such a manner that it was impossible for me to refuse.

CHAPTER TWO

I was talking about men proving their toughness in the consumption of alcohol. Mine was in a "njange" house-warming party. Our njange group consisted of the top brass of the town. If one was a man worth anything, one belonged to it.

The njange or contribution was 70.000 and the prepaid entertainment money was 5.000 francs CFA. One could as much as triple the contribution, depending on the financial power of the person whose turn it was to benefit. After all the money would be returned when one's turn came.

There was no opening for failure to contribute on a meeting day. So there was no sanction for it. Contribution was a must and a must it remained.

There were certain parameters for the party that had to follow the financial business of the day.

On top of this list were the quantity and quality of food and then drinks. It was the Chief Whip's duty to examine the food and drinks to be sure the mandatory minimum had been provided.

The group met every first Saturday of the month. The fifty strong were allowed to come along with their wives and two grownup children as their guests.

These grownup children often turned out to be a host of gatecrashers who simply walked in or could find members to usher them in. No one ever checked.

It was the event of the month in town and the envy of any important persons who could not be part of it.

A review of the events of that particular evening often went through my mind as if I was watching a film. We put ourselves through torture in the name of enjoyment.

While people in parts of East Africa and the Sudan were dying from emptiness of stomach and eating all kinds of vegetation to survive we were dying from overstuffed stomachs and throwing up to survive.

Yet everyday we filled up to above the brim, letting our cups run over.

At the meeting, as usual, each member put his money for the contribution and entertainment on the table.

The contribution money would go to the host of the day and the entertainment money would be given to the next host.

In the last meeting it had been decided that, since there would be a banquet for house-warming at the next host's house, we would have only three items on the agenda: the prayer, handing over of the two sums of money and then feasting till kingdom come.

I spent quite some time arguing with my wife about her attending the meeting. She said she could not come because she had to attend a very important meeting of Baptist women. She is an austere Born Again Christian of the Baptist Church and I am a Roman Catholic renegade.

I used to tell her I was a Born a Third Time Christian until the day she drew blood from my head with the pointed high heel of her shoe.

That evening, in her absence, I could take a few liberties. That would be the silver lining in the cloud.

I was a little late and missed a part of the prayer. I put my money silently into the hands of the Treasurer and, as Publicity

Secretary to the group, sat in my empty seat beside him at the high table.

Before long it was time for blessing the contribution money prior to its being handed over to the host.

The Chief Whip, who also sat beside me, got people to be quiet by simply calling out "Ladies and Gentlemen" with a little inflection indicative of the possible punishment of a fine in case of disobedience.

Members were apprehensive of the great increase in the fines for disturbance which took effect from the meeting in session.

The fine for unruly behaviour had skyrocketed from 500 to 1000 francs to be paid to the Chief Whip on the spot without demur.

The President stood up, tipping the table forward with his expansive belly. There was dignity in his great size.

With short stubby fingers he caressed his navel through his shirt, looking round at members amiably under the fluorescent electric bulbs.

He said he would not waste words on the money for entertainment. Spotting the next host, he threw the envelope to him.

The latter caught it expertly in the air, drawing calls of "money eye, money eye" from down the hall.

The Chief Whip stood up menacingly.

The President cleared his throat in the silence that followed. He put both palms face down on his beloved belly and took the wad of notes the Treasurer was holding out to him.

He then squeezed himself through the space between his chair and the table and, formally and ceremoniously, went round to every member with the bank notes held out in his right hand.

Each member blew a blessing onto the money and the President went on to the next one. In this manner he got to every member in the large overcrowded hall. It took time.

When he was once more at his seat, he raised the notes to his mouth. The hall burst into clapping. When it died down, he blew his own blessing on the fat wad and beckoned to the wife of the host to come forward.

She was rather shy in obeying the summons. She stood humbly in front of him and curtsied. I watched with admiration.

The President returned her greeting with a shallow bow. He tapped on the notes briefly with the tips of his fingers as if he was working on a typewriter.

"Madam," he said loudly in his deep strong voice. "Here is a penny which the men of this august group have contributed. It is for family progress. Not for drinks. Not for clothes. Not for food.

"The superintendent has more than provided money for all that already. When we next come here, you will either show us the double of what I am giving you or another fine house to warm. Here you are. Thank you."

The lady of the house flexed her knees once more after taking the notes in both hands.

With her head bowed, she walked respectfully out with the money held against her bosom. It was one million francs.

She would keep it for her husband and give him in private.

A voice called from the middle of the hall.

"Great! Everybody clap for that."

There was thunderous applause. The Chief Whip shot into the air. He glared towards the middle of the hall at no one in particular.

Silence immediately gripped the audience. He stood transfixed for a second. Then an enigmatic smile brightened his face.

"You're forgiven," he said resignedly to the hall in general. "This time."

He sat down. The hall clapped at length.

The President went back to his seat. There followed an uncomfortable spell of inactivity. Then he signalled to the host to come to the high table.

They whispered to each other for a few seconds. The President's vigorous nodding showed that an agreement had been reached.

The host went to the middle of the hall. He had an announcement to make.

"Mr. President," he said with a bow. "The high table, fellow members,   ladies and gentlemen. We have come to item eleven even though the agenda for today has only three. I want to assure you that there are enough edibles and drinkables for everybody here.

"We shall serve ourselves in the usual order. The President will lead the high table to serve themselves. Our guests shall follow. Then our wives shall lead us up. So *bon appétit* to everybody."

As if in one voice "merci" rumbled from the whole hall.

The hostess and some of the wives of members went to the great covered tables and drew the large table cloths away from the food. Exclamations of pleasure went round the hall.

Everything in the name of good food in the entire wide world seemed to be there in quantities for giants rather than ordinary human beings that we were.

Couples whose turn it was to host the group continued the strife to set a record by killing guests with food and drink.

A popular and unhealthy competition in entertainment had developed over the years as hosts strove to beat all previous records of lavish entertainment during their turn.

I was the exception to this unwritten rule. My religious wife made sure that we provided only the barest minimum each time we received the group.

She did extremely well to tolerate the consumption of alcoholic drinks inside our house.

She oversaw how people served themselves food and openly frowned at overloaded plates to the consternation of members. They would rather she sat like the women in other houses instead of standing at the dining table watching every action of theirs as if they were secondary schoolchildren in a boarding school..

Members also complained of early closing from my house. Our parties were supposed to be as close to TDB (till daybreak) as possible. At mine closure was at 1 a.m. latest.

My wife had a way of making the group disperse early without saying a word. I would have given my entertainment money to know what the others thought of us. What she did made sense anyway.

I was in for a shock when I got to the food on the tables. A feeling of being full pushed a belch into my mouth.

Constipation raised its ugly head in my stomach at the thought of going for more when everybody would have served themselves.

I counted a dozen different kinds of meat besides all kinds of vegetables, cookies, bread, rice, yam, potatoes, garri, spaghetti, several kinds of fufu, ripe and unripe plantains, stew, pepper soup and all what not.

Every guest was supposed to serve himself a piece of each kind of meat! My wife had warned me about eating or drinking too much. I wished I had a second stomach.

I decided to be smart. I served myself generously with vegetables, a little spaghetti, two large rather fatty pieces of pork and a heavy breast of chicken in tomato sauce.

The fat would disturb the absorption of alcohol in the

stomach. So it would take a good number of drinks to shake me.

CHAPTER THREE

The President looked scornfully at what he thought was a pittance on my plate. I told him I was watching my weight. He patted his paunch and guffawed. His plate was presidential – more of a small tray than any plate. Half of it was full of various cuts of goat meat. He waited for me to sit down.

"You know what P.S.?" he asked me.

I turned towards him.

"I'm all ears like a donkey, Mr. President" I said.

He patted his belly with a dull sound several times.

"This," he declared, "is the graveyard of goats."

The high table laughed briefly and returned to the business of eating. While we had been away fetching food, our table had been loaded with all types of drinks.

I took a bottle of good Bordeau which one of the girls serving opened for me. Its dryness stroked my throat. My digestion was going to be assisted.

I emptied the wine before I had eaten half the food on my plate.

Champing away like a stallion, the President nodded his appreciation.

I had only the chicken breast on my plate when people began to go for more food. The President pushed another Bordeau against my plate.

To make sure I drank it, he stood up and opened it with

the corkscrew on his penknife.

The chicken was good. I took my time over it. By the time I was putting the last morsel into my mouth, the second bottle of wine was finished.

The Chief Whip held both his thumbs up for me. The President nodded.

The host came up to the high table holding a bottle of Moët champagne in each hand. He struck the table hard with the one in his right hand.

The hall burst into clapping. He took a step to the right of the table where I was sitting.

I looked away, hoping he would not involve me in any popping of champagnes. He did. He raised both his arms into the air.

"Two guns!" he shouted. "The first for the lofty ideas and activities of our njange group and the second to drive away the cold and bad spirits from this hut that the group has enabled me build."

The voice the Chief Whip had forgiven earlier on was just waiting for that kind of opening.

"Clap for that!" he cried.

The clapping shook the foundation of the house. The President made a sign for me to stand and pop first. I did not have anything to say. I stood up and simply popped the champagne. The hall gave me a round of applause

The Chief Whip relieved me of the bottle, poured me a full glass despite my protestations. He served the high table and then went down the hall serving the anxious populace.

The President was wagging his forefinger vigorously as he stood up to open his own champagne. There was quiet.

"Don't let your hand linger there after you have cleaned it," he said. "You might touch a stinking thing. This is not a speech-making occasion. It is one for enjoyment. What I've said, I've said. What I've not said has been understood. The cup of my happiness runneth over."

"And we shall dwell in alcohol for the rest of our lives."

The voice could not have missed such a golden opportunity. The Chief Whip stopped his sharing.

"Another one," he said in anger, "and you will pay a fine."

The President shot his own gun. The hall gave him a standing ovation. The host took the bottle from him. He served the shooter first.

Down the hall I could see the Chief Whip sharing my own champagne. My hand only went twice to my lips for the full glass of champagne to vanish.

The President slammed an unopened bottle of Gordon's Gin on the table in front of me. He raised a finger of warning when I started to protest. I opened it, served myself half a glass and pushed the bottle in his direction.

He served himself copiously and pushed the bottle against the Chief Whip's plate.

I felt trouble begin to worm its way into my head. I was already feeling light. I had to stop it. When I finished the gin, I put my glass upside down on the table.

I waved a dismissing hand at the President's joking glare. My telephone showed fifteen minutes short of midnight.

The essentials of the party were over. Jokes and wisecracks were exhausted. The impromptu dancing that the host had introduced for the house-warming had gone lame.

Although there was still a lot of food, only drinking seemed to attract the guests. All these signs showed me it was time to leave. "Go while the going is good" is my motto at these moments during such occasions.

My condition was worsening as my stomach slowly absorbed

the poison. I had to leave before it got too difficult for me to find my way out of the house with dignity.

At midnight I got to my feet and squared my shoulders conspicuously. Everybody in the group knew I always made it home in my car no matter how much I had drunk.

That day they thought I had not drunk very little because I was leaving so early. They all gawked at me.

A squat man at the left of the door, with a red feather in his black raffia cap, tapped his gourd cup three times and looked in my direction.

I did not care to find out what he was trying to tell me. Witchdoctors were often gatecrasher at our meetings purportedly to take care of any instances of inebriation. This one probably wanted me to serve him a drink from the high table.

He would wait for a long time.

The fellows charged heavily for their treatment. None of them had ever come to my assistance because there had never been the need.

With one or two members, it was a regular affair. They took a helping of the palm oil concoction of the doctors virtually every meeting.

I said goodbye to the exco and was elbowing my way out on the clean floor tiles when the host caught sight of me.

He abandoned a seemingly interesting conversation with the bald director of the government hospital in town and hurried over to meet me.

I was making a great effort to stay on my feet. My head was whirling. What I would have loved most at that moment was to sit down. If I stood for long, I would simply collapse. Word would get to my wife and she would die from the disgrace.

The host stood looking down at me from his superior height. He patted me on the back.

"Levinus Kwi Kwi Kwi," he said, putting rebuke in his voice.

"I'll soon Kwi Kwi Kwi you," I replied.

"You can't do that to me!"

"Do what Superintendent? Kill myself with food and drink?"

"A few more drops of gin won't kill you. Nor will two more leaves of lettuce or a slice of chicken. Come on buddy."

"No no!"

"The night is still young, Kwi Kwi Kwi. Have one for the ditch, fellow."

I turned towards the door.

"No ditch for me," I snarled back without bitterness. "Have it on my behalf if you care."

"I don't care. I'll do same at yours, Levinus Kwinkam. I'll neither eat nor drink."

I laughed in my mind. Who was talking? That fellow who had finished a whole bottle of Scotch and half a brandy in addition to four beers when the group was last at mine.

Where would he keep his hollow leg be when they next came to mine? He was as nice a man as policemen get to be and had always had a certain liking for me. I would if I could avoid hurting him but I could not.

My body was now half blocking the doorway. I turned round in feigned anger.

"Go to hell!"

"Please beau. Don't spoil my party."

"I can't. Just let me be. I'm finished."

"You need a witchdoctor?" he asked cynically.

"Shut up!" I was wasting energy when I was in dire need of it.

"At yours I shall leave after thirty minutes. Just you wait."

The President's wife materialized beside him. He turned

to look at her and I stepped outside.

"Good night overgenerous big boy," I called over my shoulder. "My turn is light years away. You'll wait for long."

"You think I'll forget? You – "

And the President's wife pushed his face away from looking in my direction with the tips of her fingers on his temple.

Outside a quarrelling couple was so involved in their exchange that they did not realise that one could only go past by forcing one's way between them.

The woman was a dwarf beside her husband but that did not daunt her. She raised herself on her high-heeled shoes to drive home her points.

My brief wait did not mean anything to them. I squeezed through the improper fraction and stepped on the gravel of the yard.

The loud irate sigh from the small woman was meant to finish me.

I heard members calling me all kinds of names from inside. They sounded hurt. Smiling sardonically to myself, I took a few steps forward and stood to take control of my swaying body and spinning head.

I was hurrying as best I could towards where I had parked in the vast courtyard when I heard footsteps behind. Somebody was following me.

It was the hostess.

"Levy," she said. "Please take this to Madam."

She gave me something that was obviously a bottle of drink wrapped in a newspaper.

I grabbed it and stuck it in my left armpit.

"Thanks, May."

"Levy?"

"Yes?"

"Drive carefully."

"You're still a darling."

"You bet, but the hands of the clock move in one direction only."

"I've known that a long long time. Good night."

"Night night o."

She had been my secondary school sweetheart. That had been last century. It was all done with. Her husband knew about it and knew me too well to have any foolish thoughts.

He was really lucky and knew that I knew it. To go into the story would be to expose the fool that I once was. So I will not.

The parking lot was dimly lit. I made out my white Toyota Camry beside a cypress tree some thirty yards away. I wondered whether that was really where I had parked it.

The beautiful night helped my morale and jugged my memory. It was cool and dark with no moon but plenty of twinkling stars assisted by the incandescent lights of the lot.

There was a trace of a gentle fanning breeze that rocked eucalyptus and cypress trees and spread the refreshing fragrance of jasmine in the vicinity.

Trees looked like tall menacing ghosts, more distant than they really were. The Superintendent had chosen beautiful high-quality grounds for his house.

I staggered my way to the car in which I sat for a few minutes to clear my head and stabilize my body. It was difficult for me to locate the ignition key from my heavy bunch. At last I did. The old engine burst into life at once.

A ringing started in my head: fear of an accident. The thing I shall hate after death is a mangled body. I shall want to be whole and looking my best when I am lying in state prior to being put in a coffin.

When I sit behind the steering-wheel of my car after a

good drink the image of my battered bloody body looms up in front of me and I drive with utmost care.

CHAPTER FOUR

Although there is usually little traffic at this time of night, it is very dangerous because it is when the reckless cause accidents. They would be going home from bars or parties and drive without the necessary precaution.

My greater apprehension was what I would get from my wife for my condition. I somehow got to my neighbourhood safely, driving through the difficult centre of town.

In the bright lights of the car, I saw two garages at my house. Since it was dark, I peered into the one that looked less blurred. Luckily it was the correct one. I drove into it without much ado and yanked the handbrake lever.

Then trouble began. My head burst into a violent spin and dropped forward on the steering-wheel. I could still think a little but my body would not move. I let myself be, slumped over like a lifeless thing.

My wife must have waited for while for me to come to the door and when I did not, she gave instructions to my man to check. Like two or three times before, I had arrived at the house but did not get home.

They found me in a sorry state indeed. My limbs could not lift themselves, let alone bear the weight of their lifeless heavy master's body.

When my man opened the door of the car, my wife at first caught her breath. Then she stood there for full two minutes, glaring at me in loud violent silence through the dark.

If eyes could shoot bullets, I would have died from the many my wife shot the moment my boy opened the door of the car and the roof light showed me.

The boy took me softly by the shoulders to swing me sideways out of the car. With the most humiliating of manners, Madam took me roughly by the turn-ups of the trousers above the car pedals.

A big belch escaped from my throat and I begged God not to let me throw up there and then. That would be the end of my life.

The strong arms of my boy lifted my body from the driver's seat. My legs swung out gripped above the shoes by my wife and I was airborne briefly.

Once I was out of the car, my wife let my legs drop like a bag of refuse as she reached out and slammed the door with such force that a loose sheet of zinc rattle in the roof of the house. I cried out weakly.

Not a word came out of her. I might have to go for an overdraft in the bank to effect repairs of the damage of that morning. I stayed fearfully dump, praying that rain should not follow such loud thunder.

Madam did the rest of her loathsome work in maximum silence. It was the type of business that did not permit her to say anything in front of the servant. The appropriate time would come for her to drop the bomb.

They carried me like a corpse into the house with the most uncommon disrespect and dumped me from a height on a settee that would have done with softer cushions.

I was now fully conscious but made not a sound or movement. So far I had got away fairly lightly. Worse might be coming my way.

In the room adjacent to ours, our sons remained miraculously asleep despite the boisterous action. I heard my man lock the back door on his way to his room at the back of the house. My spouse stormed into our room, leaving the door wide open.

Then chapter one of her talk began. She enumerated all my disgraceful vices. Her voice was muffled but armed with such venom that if she had spoken over an ant it would have died instantly.

"Were they forcing things down your throat?" she asked. "You do not know when to stop? It was perhaps the first time you saw food or drink in your life. Gluttony is a sin.

"People must wonder whether I feed you. I do more than my duty as a wife – I give you three square meals a day! After the disgrace you come home to disturb my sleep. Nonsense!"

There were tears in her voice. I wished she would leave me alone. I refrained from telling her that some of her meals were round.

In her anger she said the same thing over and over again, only varying the language each time although thinking she was saying a different thing.

It was fine by me if her lectures made her feel better. The transfer of her pieces of mind to me would be hopefully curative this time.

I spent a whole hour on the chair with my body unable to obey the instructions from my brain.

The irate mother of my children was panting softly and sniffing once in a while. In other homes there would be pain killers in the cupboard for situations like mine. Not in ours. She would not hear of it.

Anyone who was taken ill naturally, went to the hospital. Artificially, he was welcome to jump to his death from the summit of the Buea Mountain, the highest point in West

Africa.

My headache worsened as my wife would not stop her prattle. More tears showed up in her voice and it had grown rough.

My nerves were in a bad way. I tried deep breathing and slowly got back to a pitiful semblance of myself.

The feeling of an unsettled stomach suddenly shook me hard. Still feeling weak, I managed to drag myself into the bathroom to forestall trouble.

I sat on the throne and sweated. Telltale spasms began to work their way upwards towards my throat.

The bathroom was spinning like a top with me in the middle. I felt so sick that I wished I were dead. Anything would be better than the nausea.

Soon I found myself in the centre of a vast universe spinning wickedly slowly. I leaned forward with my head in my palms. My elbows were on my knees which were swaying back and forth from the immense weight they bore.

The heaves came, disturbing my drowsiness. I tried to stand up but each time   dry heaves would block my throat and my weakened knees would flex, thrusting me back onto the toilet seat.

I would retch air painfully and spit out drops of disgusting sticky liquid onto the white tiled floor. All of a sudden I began to throw up most of the good things I had had at the party. It seemed as if I was going to vomit my very entrails but I was shame-proof.

At last I felt my head fall forward and drop on my chest. I fell asleep right there. Of course I did not know I had fallen asleep until I woke up from the ungainly position.

A loud snore accompanied by a soft whistle woke me. Both came from me. The whole place stank of putrefying food and drink from my stomach.

I would have been sick again had I not fought back. The smell of the bathroom was revolting.

I should clean the place before the Senior Mistress of Discipline came in for whatever reason. The boys might be another source of trouble. One of them or even both might want to use the toilet.

Where was I to get energy for such strenuous work? It would not be long before the cat was out of the bag and for years thereafter I would not have the end of the matter. It would become my wife's national anthem to be sung at least three times a day – morning, afternoon, and evening like taking medication.

My wife was right. Was I not eating humble pie and disturbing her sleep? The situation would have been worse had I not refused the superintendent's "one for the ditch". I might have already been in the mortuary.

How I would have loved to watch Madam from the nether world making a show of crying! The target of her harassment would have been gone forever. How she would enjoy people consoling her at her great loss.

The final implosion came. My stomach curved in, my shoulders sagged and my back hunched over. Tears were forced out of my eyes. My stomach went farther and farther from convex to concave.

I spent more than five minutes leaving the rest of what I had gulped down at the party on the bathroom floor.

The discharge made me feel better but my head was still spinning as if programmed. My backside was glued to the toilet while my arms hung full length down like those of a guerilla. All pride had drained out of me. Luckily I was alone.

Some stupid rat or wall gecko chose that moment to enjoy itself in the ceiling. It rolled some kind of ball from one side of the ceiling to the other, stopped a second or two and then started all over. It really irritated me. I gave it time with the hope that it would stop. It would not.

I got a rubber rag and, raising myself on my toes, struck the ceiling boards a number of times. There was noise enough to wake the dead. The creature stopped all movement for good.

I had heard the thing off and on the week before. I would put rat poison up there the next day. The brief action exhausted me and brought excruciating pain into my head. I fought the oncoming giddiness for I had urgent work to do.

Deeper apprehension gave me vim. My wife seemed to have said something after I struck the ceiling the last time. I heard her turn in bed. That meant she was not sleeping. She was probably listening to me and building up fury.

I sprang into action and spent thirty minutes scrubbing up the stinking mess in the bathroom and having a shower.

I finally brushed bits of food and the ugly taste of mixed drinks from my mouth and was ready for a clean bill of health – according to me.

I sniffed. That bathroom? It was spick and span but – I opened the window and the door and left both open for an obvious reason. The morning breeze would clear the stench out and let clean air in.

I sniffed again and gave a last critical look around. Both the window and door would have to stay open till sunrise. Clean air in, bad odour out!

I was getting better, you know. I was able to remember very important things. Let her come out and see her boy! I switched off the lights in the bathroom and went into the living room rather unsteadily, feeling clean in a dirty kind of way.

I sat on my famous settee and pondered over the ordeal of going to join my wife in our bedroom. The settee had needles.

My spouse would not want to hear of my being the first to leave the party. Had she been there she would have got us to leave much earlier. She needed to be in such places all the time to save the honour of the family.

Forgiveness was not the forte of my Baptist Born Again wife. She did not even understand the most important part of the Lord's Prayer – and forgive us our trespasses *as we forgive those who trespass against us.* Simple!

Forgive us our trespasses *the same as* – Therefore we had to have forgiveness in stock for others before daring to ask for ours. She would not forgive even in her dreams.

She certainly had been fanning her stamina to keep it up in her sleep because, once in a while, I heard "lack of self-respect", "disgrace to the family", "lack of self-control", "gluttony is a sin", "drinking alcohol and joking with serious matters of religion".

Each lecture ended with "nonsense!" I hoped something, some weird stuff had not entered my wife's little head.

I was nearly dropping dead with tiredness when I summoned enough courage to move. I kept myself upright with great difficulty and entered the bedroom like a cat, afraid to invite trouble.

Madam was still grumbling in her sleep. Sensing me she pushed her body into the wall she was facing and tried to eat it. Her body was as stiff as a corpse in rigor mortis. I did not dare say anything, go closer to her or touch her.

"Oh witchdoctor," I said in my mind. "Where are you to save me?"

I got in between the sheets beside her. It was comfortably warm. Yet sleep did not come as I expected. When it did, I slept very badly indeed.

The four times I caught myself snoring through a pounding headache or was victim of an elbow blow in the ribs only worsened my plight.

I had hardly rested when I heard the ringing of the bells in the nearby Roman Catholic Church for mass. I would have to slip out of bed with the greatest care.

Sunrise that morning had come with more of the crushing headache. I moved without moving and placed my feet on the carpet beside the bed.

My wife slept on, crushed against the wall. I went into a perfectly clean and odourless bathroom. With a shaking hand I had a quick shave and sprayed the room with air freshener before dressing and hurrying out of the house.

It would be an embarrassing situation if Madam met me. I did not want her breakfast. It would be loaded with venom from the night before. I sought peace and safety in departure for my office.

CHAPTER FIVE

I drove to the office slowly with the idea of a thick, black coffee in the cafeteria downstairs uppermost in my mind. A slice of buttered Best Bread with scrambled eggs would be fine with it.

That was all in my mind. My mouth did not water at all. The thought made my body emit a few menacing dry heaves. For a lover of food like me that presaged severe trouble.

I parked in the garage of the small printing business I ran. It was too early for anyone but the night watchman to be around. He had left before time. That was so much the better for my condition. He would have surely noticed.

I opened the main door downstairs, struggled up to my office, drew the blinds and crashed into the swivel chair after kicking the door shut. It was going to be a horrible day if I did not do something about it.

I knew what I was going to try: "clearance". It was a term used for self-reestablishment after a hangover. One used alcohol to fight alcohol.

There were a few bottles of beer in my office fridge. I took one out, a 33 Export. I opened it and gulped it down directly from the mouth of the bottle.

Most of my friends knew that in the absence of a witchdoctor, an early beer was a good way of getting rid of a hangover. It only took more time waiting for the good effects of the drink. For me it turned out to be a sad mistake.

Everybody knew, that in the absence of a witchdoctor, an early beer was a good way of getting rid of a hangover. It only took more time. For me it turned out to be a sad mistake.

At first everything was going fine. My head cooled and my body relaxed. Then, all of a sudden, the light from outside became aggressively bright. I drew the dark blue velvet curtains together. With my elbows on the table, I held my head in both palms.

I might have to send for a friend of mine who was a nurse in the Regional Hospital or, better still, a witchdoctor after all. They exercised a lot of discretion. Madness! Who was I becoming? Where was I heading?

When the telephone rang right in the middle of my head, I would have roared in rage but for fear of splitting my delicate cranium in two. I used a safe soft voice to answer.

The caller was a rich client asking for the invitation cards he had ordered for the wedding of his son. I had noticed the package at the receptionist's downstairs the day before. I directed him there for 8 o'clock.

I was just putting down the receiver when someone banged on the door with something like a sledgehammer. I was going to give the sack to the employee who dared knock on my door in that authoritative manner.

Offices opened at 8 o'clock. I put on an expression of fury for which I did not have the energy. The door knob turned and stopped.

The door itself began to open annoyingly slowly with an unusual creak. Someone was taking all the time in the world to come in.

I wanted to but could not look away from the door. I was keeping up my head with a lot of difficulty and my expression of fury must have turned into a clownish grimace of pain.

Downstairs my printing machines were making a deliberate effort to be viciously loud. The hard working printer had come in earlier and started his machines. It seemed such a wrong thing to do that morning.

A gigantic figure closed the door mercifully on their noise.

The figure strode up to my bureau. It was a warder of well over sixty years of age. His actions were slow, deliberate and annoying.

I stopped myself just in time from telling him that the Ubea Prison was on the other side of town.

What was he still doing in service at that age anyway? The sympathetic look on his old homely face neither helped my temper nor my aching head.

He stood confidently akimbo leaning his black belted waist against my bureau. He spoke English with the accent of the Kwerri tribe at the foot of the Ubea Mountain.

He seemed broader than the width of the door.

"My greetings to you," he said with calm light-heartedness.

"Yes," I answered curtly, "Can I help you?"

He did not answer at once. He was enjoying studying my condition, the result of the immoderations of my life.

I would not have been able to muster enough energy to order him out of my office. Without being invited he sat down on one of my chairs for guests.

He was big, at least six feet four inches tall and of the refined blackness of his size 14 boots. His face had a broad forehead with shaggy eyebrows under which were tiny, sharp dark brown eyes.

His nose stretched from one ear to the other. The nostrils were big and lined with grey hair. His mouth was out of pro-portion with the nose and moustache above it.

Closed it could not have measured more than one inch across but, as I found out later, it was possessed of an inexhaustible store of words.

At my scrutiny, his face lit up as if with interior light reflected by his even white teeth.

"Yes, you can help me, my son," he said with irritating unwaveringness. "But I need to help you first. That's how I am. When I see something that is not correct, I go for it like a shark."

"What's this about, Pa?"

He chuckled.

"You are ill and I know both the disease and the medicine."

His utterance nearly knocked me down. He chuckled some more. I wondered whether my condition was that obvious from my appearance.

The tall man was shaking his head rhythmically with a knowing look in his eyes.

I do not know whether it was fear or admiration that glued my attention to his face. I thought if he could, he should. My disquiet melted away.

I would have liked to say something but talk would only worsen my headache. Helpless acquiescence must have shown up in my manner of sitting. To my disappointment my collocutor just stood there looking down at me.

I feared he would stay that way till night instead of providing the promised medicine for my illness. His mouth was shaking spasmodically with amusement, ready to spray me with words. I had no choice but to hold my horse

With massive ceremony he put two thick eighty leaves exercise books on the central leather cushion on my bureau. With no less show, he took off his age-worn prison officer's cap, exposing kinky hair that was as white as cotton.

He put the cap gingerly on the exercise books and – I heard him talking from a great distance. My attention could hardly hold.

He seemed to be saying something about going to look for medicine for my sick head. I was not to move. I do not know who he thought he was to be giving me orders in that relaxed way. My retort ended at the level of intention for I did not really say anything audible.

I let my heavy head drop on the table. The pain was going in rhythm with the beating of my heart. There was silence for a long. time. When I heard his boots on the floor, I did not know whether he was leaving or had just returned.

CHAPTER SIX

All of a sudden, there he was in front of me with a handful of herbs in his big hands. An aromatic medicinal smell emanated from the freshness of the herbs.

He came round my table and took my head in big powerful hands which, I was certain, no prisoner could escape from.

He pushed my head gently against the back of the chair. I closed my eyes tightly.

The giant took the herbs in his hands and rubbed them vigorously together between his palms until they turned a limp dark green. Then he passed me an order.

"Hold your head straight up."

I obeyed him without hesitation. Somewhere deep inside my being I was displeased. I was asking myself why I was obeying orders from that strange old man. He was a warder, not a witchdoctor. I was not even totally certain of the kind of warder he was.

I had to give him and my aching head a chance. Many doubting Thomases, in the course of time, have lost a great deal through their infamous disposition.

He used his hands on my head. The palms were surprisingly soft. His hands were like shovels. The left took my head by the nape.

Armed with the crushed herbs the right, began to rub them firmly against my forehead. As the action progressed, my head began to lighten.

The warder worked for some fifteen seconds, rubbing and grinding the leaves into my very skull. The throbbing pain began to lose its force. My head grew lighter and lighter. I began to marvel at the warder/witchdoctor's magic.

He stepped back and peered at my forehead.

"Shake your head hard." he ordered.

I obeyed as much as I could. I could not continue because there was sharp pain coming from my left temple.

"Touch the area that hurts," commanded the herbalist.

I put my hand over my left temple. The warder rubbed with his herbs and I felt the area get warm.

The smell of the herbs had grown more pleasant.. A miracle was happening in my head. The pain was melting away.

"Shake your head hard once more," came the next command.

I obeyed once more. This time the pain came from the middle of my head. The witchdoctor went for it. In this manner, he chased the pain round my head with the rubbing of his herbs.

Each time the pain escaped to some other area but got duller until I felt only a tautness in my forehead. The doctor scooped up the pains with his herbs and held them up to me. I shook my head as before.

There was only a numbness that I could cope with on my left temple. No pain. I felt perfectly well.

My doctor brought the withered leaves down in front of my face.

"There's your pain in the herbs," he said. "It's invisible of course. No one can *see* pain. I'll throw everything out of the window."

He opened the window and put his words into action, blocking a protest in my throat. I was very strict about littering around my establishment.

"Please –" I started.

He did not listen to me for it seemed he had something important to tell me.

"If someone picks up those herbs and touches his forehead with them," he declared, "all your headache will immediately go to him."

I nodded my comprehension and acquiescence. My face was warm and damp. I dabbed it with my handkerchief. The old man was watching me with a sleepy expression.

On each of his meaty shoulders were the three stripes of a senior warder grade one. In the police the rank would be sergeant.

"How did you do it?" I wanted to know.

A mischievous smile smoothened the wrinkles on the warder's face.

"My son," he replied, "do you want to know everything in the world?"

"I'm only asking," said I.

"Leave that to me. Let me also know this thing that you don't know. From your education you know so many more things than I."

I shrugged.

"Okay. What do I do now to compensate you for your medicine."

"My word! You educated people," the witchdoctor exclaimed with his moustache trembling above his small mouth. "A person mayn't help the other anymore? Everything is paid for."

"Correct in a way. Nothing should go for nothing."

"That's not the black man's way. I do you a favour and you want to pay me back so that you should not be indebted to me."

"It's only fair. A draw. One one."

"Yea that's the way of white folks. I know them very well.

I was in the Second World War with them in Burma."

"So?"

"Oh yes. We were soldier comrades. I ate with British soldiers at table. They patted me on the back and I patted them too. Forget that, fellow."

"You took care of the sick over there?"

"I'm not telling. Know this. For good to be good, it should not be paid for. I get my herbs free so you don't need to pay for them."

"You're a kind of witchdoctor?"

Anger flashed across the face of the giant. He glared at me for a second before controlling himself.

"There you go again with the unbelieving ways of the white man. Right now I'll show you the wizardry of my medicine. I'll get those herbs and rub them on your head."

He took a threatening step towards the door.

I gasped. The thought of that excruciating headache coming back weakened me at the knees. I did not want to be a guinea pig.

"No please!" I cried. "I'm sorry. Forgive me, Pa."

The traditional doctor wagged his right forefinger at me.

"Don't tease me anymore," he warned.

I feared to say anything. Without a word to me, the warder went into the toilet and washed his hands. He came out smelling of my Rexona soap and sat down.

CHAPTER SEVEN

The old man waited patiently, looking around aimlessly at things in my office while I enjoyed my new-found health and fooled around with a few old newspapers on my bureau.

When he had had enough of my tomfoolery, he pushed the two exercise books towards me. I turned them over to have a better look.

Both were dog-eared and, though they were not old, had either passed through many hands in a short time or someone had worked intensively on them within the same amount of time.

They were numbered ONE and TWO and there was a title on ONE:

THE LEGACY
RANDALL NGUBETT
(DECEASED)

I picked ONE up and opened the pages at random. It was a manuscript written in a bold, rather effeminate hand. Here was a cancellation, arrows, bubbles and page references galore.

It was going to be a tough job deciphering the information in this book which looked like some kind of autobiography since it was written in the first person.

It was obvious that the warder had not written it or had it

written. What then did he want me to do with this thing that seemed to have come right out of the grave?

There was nothing I would not have done for that doctor. He had performed a miracle on my head. He might have performed another in those exercise books. After all he had proven himself a powerful witchdoctor. I determined to find out.

I looked my gratitude into the sexagenarian's eyes and decided to humour him.

"Doctor, what do you want me to do with these exercise books?"

The doctor smiled broadly, stretching his lips to the limit. I feared for his mouth.

"Don't call me doctor, you rogue," he said chuckling. "Read what's in those exercise books, correct it and print it into books."

"Okay, Pa," said I, "I'll read it first. Then we can talk. There's a lot to discuss and sort out before we get to the stage of printing."

"Yes, I know. There's money involved. It will be taken care of."

"What I mean is −"

"You heard me. This is a printing press isn't it?"

"Yes but how many do I print? How soon? Who will pay?"

"Mrs. Ngubett the secretary of the Bokiko Town Cooperative will pay."

"Okay, that's clear. How many copies will she pay for?"

"She said she would leave the quantity to you. She'll pay for as many as you print."

"Will she?"

"I mean a reasonable number, of course, after you'd've judged the marketability."

"Who reads books these days anyway, so who buys any books at all?"

"You'll have to discuss those details with her. Money, as I said before, is not the problem. She's doing her late son's bidding,"

"Okay. It'll be her funeral."

The small mouth opened in a wry smile.

"Not yours," it said. "The writer is Mrs. Ngubett's son, the young man they killed a few weeks ago. Anyway, she said she'd be coming to see you herself tomorrow afternoon after work."

I began to tap my right foot thoughtfully on the carpeted floor. I did not want to hurt the old man. Yet I did not want to go into any risky business of printing copies of a book that no one would buy, let alone read, no matter how good it was.

I did not want to get into any kind of loss, even if it was not mine. It would likely harm my cherished baby business for a long time.

"Okay, Pa," I said at last. "I'll browse through the book and see her tomorrow."

"Good. I'm glad but – "

"Yes, Pa?"

"What I'm going to tell you now will be part of the book. I got Mrs. Ngubett's permission."

"You did?"

He ignored my question.

"Please get a pen and paper to write it down."

I was in for something. The good treatment he had given me might attract good payment in kind. The worker was entitled to his pay.

Like a little schoolboy I got ready with pen and paper for the approaching dictation.

The big warder clasped his hands and put them beside my IN-tray. Cool air was making its way past the curtains and driving my malaise farther away. The warder looked into my face to show he was ready.

"Look," he began, with the suggestion of a smile at the corners of his extraordinary mouth, "the writer of this book was executed."

I had heard about the execution. The young man was supposed to have killed his wife and the Ubea Manager of Interbank.

In the days when I was a journalist in "The Daily Express" I used to shoot out like a bullet for investigation on getting word of such happenings.

Things changed when I opened my printing and publishing business. A great deal had also changed in journalism for the one of the day was a different brand from the one we learned in the university. What we thought was sensational was now standard.

The profession had also become too attached to money for my liking. Now, journalists did not think they should waste their time on homicide cases when there were loads of money to be made from covering political campaigns and writing directed articles that fetched money from the wealthy.

As far as the case went, it seemed as if the wife had been carrying on with both the Manager of the Interbank and the young husband's best friend.

I knew the girl. Despite being the daughter of the richest man in the whole region, she was the girl for every new arrival of name in town.

When she got betrothed to a young man, it was the talk of the whole region. They were hastily married in a lavish feast to which I had been invited but could not go because I was in Nigeria to buy printing machines and materials for my printing press business.

At the time I wondered what she was offering her husband.

At the time I wondered what she was offering her husband. It was common knowledge that she was barren. Perhaps she had not been that way and people simply wanted to drag her name into mud.

Another negative against her was her evil temper outside the roving eye. If she wanted a man, she went for him and did all in her power to get him.

The old girl – she was at least five years older than her man – had disappeared from circulation for some time after marriage and people had begun to talk so well of her for having 'settled down' only for her to resurface as a corpse for an expensive coffin.

The few details I had had about the case , as I said earlier, had come from my wife who had been so interested in the matter that, for the first time in her life, she appeared in court.

For weeks on end Ubea had been full of talk of what everybody called 'the gruesome Killings of Bonaberi Quarters'.

My wife told me the court was packed full everyday of the hearing. She told me that on the day judgment was passed, everybody who was anybody in Ubea was in court.

Well, I had not been in court. Therefore I was nobody according to her. She would be surprised on seeing the whole story being offered me on a platter of gold.

CHAPTER EIGHT

The warder brought me back to the present with the authority he used on prisoners.

"Get ready to write," he ordered with quiet assuredness.

I came out of my daydreaming.

"I'm ready," I said, avoiding the least show of resentment in my voice.

"You're ready to write?"

"Yes, Pa."

"Remember to write down everything. Leave nothing out."

I was getting impatient with the fellow's anxiety to make everything more than crystal clear.

"That's what I'll do, Pa."

"Alright, start writing."

My visitor pushed himself farther over the leather pad on my bureau. He screwed up his eyes with their shaggy brows and was peering short-sightedly right into my warm brain. I was afraid that if I looked closer into his big hairy nostrils I would see his epiglottis.

"Write that my son who is in college has read that book to me. I know all that is inside it. Write."

He leaned back from my bureau and stretched his feet out in front of me to relax as I was writing. "Are you already through?"

I ignored his surprise. His brows drew together.

"You write a lot faster than my boy who is in college. And

that boy of mine writes like a typewriter."

I realised that he thought I had not been to college. His son was there.

"I do my best, Pa."

"Alright, you've written that my son has read that book to me and I know all that is in it?"

"Yes, I have."

"Write that I'm an old man but I'm neither a thief nor a liar. Write."

I wrote it down. The warder watched my pen as if he could read every word that flowed out of it.

"Man, you really are educated! Alright, I'm not a liar. I'm not a thief. Write that I did not go to school but I'm very intelligent. I'm even more intelligent than a lot of people who say they went to school. Write."

My companion thrust himself forward and peered at the page as if he could read what I was writing.

"I'm through,"

"Are you sure you're writing well?" he asked with his brows still drawn together.

"I sure am."

"Alright. I said my son had read all that is written in the book to me. I don't lie and I don't steal. I also said I didn't go to school but I'm more intelligent than many people who have gone to school. You've written all that down?"

I looked perfunctorily over what I had written.

"Everything's in there, Pa."

"Read it all back to me."

I thought the temptations of man on earth were limitless. Pa sat back and listened to me as I read aloud all he had dictated.

He understood English perfectly well, having, as he had said, fought alongside British soldiers in Burma during the

Second World War. They shared camaraderie. A little grin appeared below his moustache.

"Had your house been near mine," he said, "you'd have been writing my letters for me. You've written all that has come out of my mouth faithfully."

I wanted him to get to the end of what he wanted me to write. I had a lot of work pending. I might think of becoming his letter writer some day.

"Write that to go to school is not to become intelligent and being intelligent is not from going to school. A man mustn't go to school to be intelligent and going to school doesn't give a man intelligence. Intelligence comes from God."

I wrote as fast as I could, knowing that I would have to read it all back to him. I did not want to scrutinize the sexagenarian's thoughts or philosophy of life.

What disturbed me were the unending repetitions and verifications. It would be nightfall before we were done.

"I told you that the man who wrote this book was hanged," the old man went on. "Before he was executed, he took many a day to write this book. He thought I could promise him a thing and fail to do it.

"That was a lie. I am not like that. Lies are for the young of today, not the old like us. When I promise to do a thing, I do it to the best of my ability. No less. Write that down."

I ignored what he said about the writer being dead and wrote down the rest as best I could.

"Write that it is good for an intelligent man to seem foolish. There are times when a man may be intelligent, show it and die through it.

"Other times, ill luck may meet him without his knowing its origin. The boy who was executed had intelligence but was dogged by ill luck even though –"

The old man was overestimating my speed of writing.

"Slow down a little, Pa," I said, "so that I can finish writing."

"Sorry, I got carried away."

I finished writing and looked up.

"At first the boy talked of paying me for the work I was going to do. I did not say anything. The day he started writing a note to his mother to give me an advance, I nearly struck him with my truncheon. Write."

I scribbled away.

"Done," I told the warder.

"Where was I? Yes. That day, he looked at me for a long time. I mean the day he wanted to write to his mother to give me money. Then he laughed with pleasure. He took my hand in his chained one and shook it hard. He talked to me for a long time. I could not stop the tears flowing down my old cheeks. I – "

He was talking too fast again.

"Pa stop!" I cried.

"Okay."

I wrote furiously.

"I'm through."

"He gripped my hand. He told me he would remember me as a friend wherever he went after death. I was moved. I burst into tears like a little girl. We grabbed each other and wept together.

"Hey man, you will teach my son who is in college to write as fast as you. You follow one's words with the pen as they come out of the mouth."

An idea occurred to me.

"Pa, why don't you tell me all that you want me to write at once? I'll keep it in my head and write it all down after. Then read it all back to you to check."

He shook his mighty head.

"Why? I've finished? Not much left. Write this. It's okay that they killed that boy but I don't think a woman has the right to refuse to bear children for her

husband as the wife did.

"If she could not have children, she should have told her husband so that he could marry another woman to bear him children. She should not have shared her barrenness with him. That's plenty. Write."

So the author's wife had refused to have children. How could she have refused to have a thing that was impossible for her to have?

She had long destroyed her body and must have pretended to be on the pill.

The better of the evils was to deceive her husband and the world instead of being known to be unproductive.

The husband must have had vain hopes of having children. The old warder was quiet. He seemed to have at last had his say and was giving me all the time I wanted to finish writing the last thing he had said.

I put a full stop with a stabbing action of my ball point pen and summoned his attention.

"I think you've now finished, Pa."

"Sonny, does one ever finish talking? The day you are buried is the day you stop talking. Finished. Discussion was once so interesting that a few friends and I talked till the next morning. I'm telling you. I'll soon finish and let you go on with your work."

CHAPTER NINE

I was depressed. He still had a mighty lot to say. He would never finish and leave. He continued to talk.

"One important thing more" he took up his talk again. "Talk to Mrs. Ngubett when she comes to see you this afternoon. Console her. Death is death no matter its manner. There is no good one. No bad one. I will now tell you an important part of the story."

I nearly collapsed from sheer frustration which I would not show. The fellow was going to say something more to take up some more of my precious time. My patience would not last forever.

"What is it now, Pa?" It was hard for me to keep impatience out of my voice.

"This is how I think it all happened. Young Ngubett killed two people and yet he did not kill anyone. Don't laugh. It is not a laughing matter. He loved that artificially light-skinned woman to a finish.

"That did not stop her from continuing to have men outside. Habits die hard. When you move a dog from a place, it is only the place you have changed, not the dog. It remains the dog of old."

I grudgingly saw what he meant.

"The woman went on chasing trousers after marriage. She did not spare her husband's best friend who was more of a brother. Before marriage she had spoilt her womb with her bad behaviour."

"Am I to write that too?"

"Have it your way now. Keep it all in your head and fix it after I have left."

"Okay. Pa."

"There was this old white man with a strong cough whose mistress she had been for many years. He was the expatriate agric. officer for Ubea. When she got the illness from him, she coughed blood and became as thin as this little finger of mine.

"We thought she would die. Dr. Ngan, her father's best friend did wonders for her. Her father's money saved her life. She got well in a way, a way to be a trap to anyone who struck her. I'm sure that's what happened for her to die. She provoked young Ngubett into striking her and he carried ill luck that paved the way to his grave.

"We had all thought she would never marry. Now, out of the blues came young inexperienced Ngubett, easy fish for the old girl. He was employed in the same office in which she worked. She went to work on him and the boy's head spun like a top.

"She caught him like a cat catches a mouse. He went straight for marriage. Her father took a fortune for her bride-price and hurried things up for them to wed before the boy could find out the truth."

My fingers were weary for the work was taking too long.

"So they got married. He caught her in infidelity and killed her?" I asked, hoping to bring the story abruptly to an end.

"Not so fast," the witchdoctor replied. "The girl had hot blood that could not be cooled in a day, a week or even a month of married life. At first she seemed happy and satisfied to have married such a handsome intelligent young man, so much younger than her.

"Soon the force of her previous life descended on her and she went back to her old ways and former male friends. I swear to God that no son of mine shall ever marry a rich man's daughter!"

I wondered why the old boy was telling me his version of the story when the original one was in the exercise books in front of me.

He ought to let me get it directly from the author. I was not going to publish the story twice over. I stifled a yawn and showed him listening interest on my face.

"You have a good reason," I mumbled.

"Did the marriage last?" the witchdoctor continued with a rhetorical question. "Where? It ended in two deaths – that of the woman and her old bank manager boyfriend.

"How could death result from a weak blow to the woman's chest? Dr. Ngan carried out a post mortem on her body but no word was ever heard of it. Man, it's time for me to go back to my job site."

He stood up suddenly with his cap in hand? I put my pen down and stood up too. He straightened his stiff, starched uniform and marched to the door the handle which he took in his big right hand.

I followed him to the door. He yanked it open and held out his hand. Mine completely disappeared in the shovel. I was glad he did not squeeze as I might have obtained multiple fractures.

"Thank you very much, Pa," I said with a bow over his hand.

"Whatever for?"

"The work on my head and the business you've brought me."

"Don't mention. It's been a pleasure. Bye."

"Bye, Sir."

He strode onto the landing with his size 14 boots and unintentionally slammed the door. He thought nothing of it and continued his way.

I was happy to be out of my hangover. The old witchdoctor's unending talk though boring, was nothing juxtaposed with my headache.

I now understood why some of the members of my njange group were great customers to witchdoctors. Mine was one with a difference for he worked gratis. I went back to my swivel chair.

CHAPTER TEN

I left the office two hours after closing time. I had read through a reasonable part of the first of the two exercise books which made up the manuscript of "THE LEGACY".

I drove speedily home with the intention of resting and continuing work. I parked the Camry in the garage, expecting my boys to dash out to welcome me. No such thing happened. They were surely away from home.

As I walked into the house I smelt my favourite meal – fried ripe plantains, white beans and huckleberry in tomato sauce with chopped half-cooked carrots. I went straight to the dining-room.

My wife had left a note beside a covered glass bowl with a slice of avocado. She had taken the boys with her to a church meeting. There was also a three-quarter-full bottle of wine on the table.

I recognised the wrapped gift of the night before from May. My wife had drunk some of the wine!

I enjoyed what was obviously a meal of reconciliation, washed it down with half of the wine left and crashed into my famous settee of the night before for siesta.

I was awoken some thirty minutes later by my man throwing things about in the kitchen. I went into my study with the manuscript, locked the door and started reading.

I came out when I heard my wife and boys returning from

their meeting. The boys were all over me. Ruxon, ten, gave me a few painful punches on my navel and Jock, four, wanted a ride on my shoulders.

My wife controlled them, telling them to leave me alone since I was tired from work. She asked me how my lunch had been. I raised my right thumb. She smiled and went into the kitchen to make us tea.

After tea I told her to forget about supper for me. I was not hungry and had work I had to finish before going to bed. She understood. By midnight I had finished the first exercise book.

The next day I finished the second one at 11 a.m. in the office. Then I sent for my accounts clerk and we worked out how much it would cost to produce a thousand copies of the book. We arrived at 550,000 francs.

The amount would be within reach of the person the warder had described. I would see.

I intended to go out before closing time so I told the accounts clerk to watch out for a certain Mrs. Ngubett. If she called in my absence, he was to ask her for a fifty per cent advance on the cost of printing a thousand copies of her book. The advance would make me know how serious she was.

At 1530 I was closing the door of my office for early departure home when she arrived. I opened the door for her and showed her the chair the old witch-

doctor had sat on the day before.

She ran both her hands down her rear and sat down. She must have been a great number when she was young. Even now, in the wrong side of forty, she was something to look at.

She was medium all round – head, height, bust, hips and legs. Grief had given her a haggard look but she could still smile sweetly.

She wore an expensive French perfume that embellished

my office. Everything about her sparked of class and quiet efficiency.

She was not a person to waste time so she went straight to what had brought her to my office. I was going to find out why they had chosen me for their book issue.

"I'm Mrs. Ngubett," she said without ceremony. "You talked with Pa Kumbat, didn't you Mister – ?"

"Kwinkam, Levinus Kwinkam, Mom."

"He was here yesterday morning, I believe Mr. Kwinkam." She was not asking. She was telling me.

"Levinus, Mom, no formality for me," I replied, putting finality in my voice and giving it a few seconds to sink in properly. "Yes, Mom, we discussed for long."

I so much regarded the lady as a mother that any formality with her would have hurt.

"How many copies are we printing, Levinus?" she asked. The lady was sharp. The hint had gone through.

"I thought one thousand copies would do for now. It'll be a trial run. Later, depending on the sales, we could do more."

"You will do the editing, won't you, Levinus? I hear you used to be a great journalist…"

"Well, I did my best but did not want to continue with the profession."

"I know you'll polish up the English."

"I've already browsed through. I'll do the last reading on the typed copy."

"How nice! How much will everything cost?"

"Five hundred and fifty thousand francs but you can pay a half now and the other half on delivery."

"Never mind. I may as well pay everything right away. It comes to the same thing in the end. Just give it your best, Levinus."

"Sure, Mom."

She cocked her head to one side.

"When the printing is done, we'll discuss the sales. Call me then."

"I'll work it out and we can do the finishing touches together."

"That'll be nice of you Levinus. You needn't be afraid of anything. I'll pay for all your expenses."

"I understand that much, Mom, but money is not of all importance to me. There are other values in life."

She studied my face for a spell. Her eyes had dark shadows under the lower lids. Her grief had been profound. She reached for her handbag on my bureau and hesitated as if she was waiting for somebody or something.

High quality showed all over the light green leather of her handbag. I got a glimpse of her shoes of the same colour. She was a woman of taste.

"Your mind is the same like that of my late son, Levinus. You're of the same school of thought."

"An honour, Mom," I replied with a certain tightness in my throat, "to be like a man I've developed admiration for from reading his manuscript."

She nodded, lowering her eyelids with long eyelashes.

"Thank you," she said in a near whisper. The trace of a smile swept across her melancholic face.

"If there's anything I can do anytime – "

She took a brown cheque-book from her handbag and, in a clear cursive hand, wrote out a cheque for five hundred and fifty thousand francs. She crossed it neatly without the use of a straight edge and held it out to me. I took it with my right hand, stood up and bowed my thanks.

She took her handbag and stood up to leave. I came round

my bureau and led her to the door, remembering what the witchdoctor-warder had told me.

She did not resist when I took her hand. I held it firmly and led her out of the office door.

"Mom," I said. "I know what happened. Please take heart. Leave everything in the hands of the Almighty."

A low sniff came from her nose. I looked down at her face, afraid that my sympathy had touched her to the quick. She was not weeping.

I held her hand for a little longer. I felt my reassurance take effect. As she went out of the door she looked up into my face with motherly gratitude.

"You are very kind, my son. That's the way I already feel towards you. God bless you. Don't follow. You have so much work to do. Bye."

"I'll keep you posted on how the work is going."

"No need to. I know so little about such things. Just get it done. I trust you. Levinus."

"Thanks, Mom."

"Don't mention."

The sound of her footsteps cleared the landing and began to go down the stairs. I closed my office door soundlessly. I had found myself a mother.

My blood one had died when I was still an infant. This one was the kind of person with whom I liked to do business. I resolved to give her more than her money's worth.

I went downstairs to talk to my editor-in-chief. Work was to begin immediately on the manuscript. All overtime work would be paid to the last franc.

The secretary would start typing the manuscript that very evening and do nothing else until it was finished.

The printer would start printing the book as soon as the

secretary and editor-in-chief were done. I would get a few of my former colleagues to do reviews of the book in their newspapers. I was going to recommend a book launch after which sales would begin.

I visualized the kind of happiness I would bring into my mother's life. The witchdoctor too would be happy and talk unendingly about the book. The problem was where I was to insert what he had dictated to me. I could not see where. I had to be careful with that witchdoctor.

That night the solution to the problem came to me. THE LEGACY would be published after it had been introduced in a short story in which the witchdoctor-warder's story would feature. On learning about the matter the old man's mouth would stretch dangerously to its very limits in a big smile.

THE LAST HUNT

EXCERPT FROM THE NOVEL, "THE GUN"

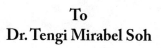

To
Dr. Tengi Mirabel Soh

CHAPTER ONE

Thecla Ado and I were living in a state of war in one compound. The gun my identical twin brother had left on dying was the main bone of contention. There were many other issues we would have disagreed on had the gun not preoccupied both our minds so much. It was the first thing on my mind every time I saw her and I did all I could to meet her as few time as possible.

I felt the anger and deep animosity in her eyes each time she stood looking down towards my house without knowing whether I was in or not. And this was often.

If she could, she would have willed me to death but, unfortunately for her, she could not and I was too much on my guard for her to use the direct method she had used on my brother.

I knew she thought the firearm was not more mine than theirs, despite its being in my keeping, since I was not using it and could not dispose of it any way I wanted. The idea annoyed me.

I took a decision to go hunting with the firearm to prove my ownership to her. She would watch me walk past my brother's villa with her mouth watering in anticipation for game she would think I was going to share with her.

I would walk past her with a swagger and, on reaching my house, call out loudly to my wife to come and help me with the heavy bag of meat.

I went to bed fairly early that evening determined to carry out my resolution the next morning. I had slept for less than two hours when I had a horridly vivid dream.

My brother appeared to me. He was coming rather belatedly for I had thought he would make contact with me within a few days after his burial.

In the dream he stood at the door and refused to come into my house. In anger he accused me of spurning his property and disobeying the instructions he had given before dying.

In our custom to spurn a dead person's property is to refrain from taking possession of it and putting it to appropriate use.

Both Kang's imaginary wife and the gun were part of his property. I was supposed to marry his wife and hand over the gun to his brother-in-law.

Marry who? Thecla Ado! Me? Hand over what? That gun! The baloney! Why did he not come out of the grave and make me do his bidding? Rubbish!

In the dream Kang asked me what type of brother I thought I was. He spoke in our native tongue to make the effect more poignant.

I was touched to the quick. He was forgetting how, long ago, in a conspiracy with our parents, he had replaced me, the better candidate for being sent to secondary school. He dared talk to me that way from the grave.

I sprang to my feet to confront him. Looking directly into his eyes, I asked him what kind of brother he thought he was. Would he like to tell me what right he had to order the family gun to be given to his brother-in-law?

If the funny fellow owed him, he should have told me. Since the latter had not publicly announced the debt while he lay in state, it meant there was no such thing as a debt. Why was he then disturbing me?

He still claimed to be the elder of us two! I used to smile sardonically at the idea of 'an elder brother' with identical twins born on the same day with perhaps less than fifteen minutes between their births.

I told him I would not give the gun to Alemnus. His supposed wife could go and commit suicide by hanging from the mango tree behind his villa.

He suddenly lunged at me and I must have cried out in my sleep. The nightmare woke me and I sat up in bed with my heart pounding against my rib cage as if it would crack it. Light from the security electric bulb outside reached my room dimly through the window. The shadowy presence at my door was definitely an illusion. I wiped cold sweat from my brow.

I started when I heard soft barefooted footsteps crossing the living room towards my room. I breathed with relief when I realised that it was only the Mother of Ache probably coming to find out what the matter was.

As she came into my room. There was no need acting as if nothing had happened. She had heard me cry out in my sleep.

She shook me unnecessarily violently on my right shoulder.

"What's the matter the Father of Ache?" she asked, breathing hard in perturbation.

"You find me awake and you still shake me? It was only a dream," I replied, lying down once more and pulling the blanket up to my chin to keep warm.

"Tell me about it."

"No. Tomorrow. Go back to sleep, please."

"But it is already tomorrow, the Father of Ache."

"So?" I asked. "Never mind. Please go back to bed."

She did not raise her voice but insisted powerfully in the way only women can.

"Do tell me the Father of Ache," she pleaded. "It will come

out of your mind and not repeat itself."

"Didn't you hear me?" I asked touchily. "I said tomorrow whenever it is. Go back to sleep, please."

She sighed and purposefully shuffled back to her room. She must have fallen asleep immediately. I could not do like her.

I lay awake disturbed by thoughts. So, since both Kang's imaginary wife and the gun were part of his property, he and custom would have me inherit her also.

CHAPTER TWO

I was tossed and turned continuously until I heard a cock crow somewhere in the neighbourhood. It was time for action.

My resolve to go hunting was so strong that I could sense the ambience of the forest and hear the gurgling of a brook, the twitting of birds and the cries of wild animals in my mind while I was still in bed.

I was neither going to hand the gun over to Thecla Ado's brother nor marry her. If Kang came out of the grave in his body to tell me, I would only then do his bidding.

Kang could not do anything about the gun where he was. I could do as I liked with it here. It belonged this way. Not there across the bar. The gun was now fully mine alone and mine it would remain.

After that thought, the notion of hunting gripped me with even greater urgency. It developed fast and the desire grew into a veritable palpable drive. Bush meat for the house for a change from the daily beef or frozen fish became a pressing need.

Towards sunrise I felt good in anticipation of the hunting sport. I got out of bed at 5.15 when it was still quite dark outside. My hunting would be a lot more than just hunting. It would be some kind of pleasurable revenge.

I would get game and take sadistic pleasure in the anger that my action would stir up in my gigantic sister-in-law by assertion. She would crave for a piece of meat from what I would shoot.

I would make sure she saw what I brought back. I knew how she adored meat. Not a morsel would she taste. Hard luck for her!

She would definitely complain to her flat-footed brother, telling him how I was still keeping the gun and had had the effrontery to go hunting with it. He would know once and for all that the gun was mine and would never be his.

I got dressed for action. Resplendent in fatigues I had bought in the area of second-hand clothes in the quarter marketplace, I did a little jogging on the spot in my room to invigorate my body and boost my morale. After that I was ready.

I took down the gun from its new place of storage – on a metal hook on the wall in my bedroom – and pulled it out of its polished, sophisticated brown leather sheath.

I cleaned it to my heart's satisfaction. An unloaded test for efficiency showed it ready to go. As it was, so was I, I thought.

I looked around for my hunting bag. There were four cartridges left in it. My wife should know where it was. I hated to disturb her sleep a second time but I had to if I was to find the bag quickly and get to the forest at the appropriate time.

I asked her across the sitting room and, light sleeper that she was, she immediately told me. I pulled it out from under my bed. Custom did not permit me to tell anyone that I was going hunting. That was supposed to bring ill luck.

Since my wife was aware of my intention, I might as well postpone the trip and leave before dawn the next day. To hell with the exacting demands of tradition! I was not going to postpone that hunting trip.

If I did not go that morning, I would lose doubly in not having bush meat to eat in my house and so not being able to provoke the famous widow. I would also be plagued all day long by the feeling of having failed to do an important activity. I had to go.

Ache was saying something. He seemed to be trying to get down from his mother's bed. He was strong of will like people said I had been at his age. Let him wait till I took it out of him. I would give him what my father had given me to take out what I had brought from my mother's womb.

"Stop that nonsense out there, Ache," I growled, "or I'll come and give you hot pepper to eat right away."

His mother must have pushed him farther onto the bed. I got my things together quickly and sneaked out, leaving my wife to solve the Ache problem.

I went up the slope past Kang's villa, now mine of course, in the fading darkness and ascended the steep hill on the eastern side of the quarter.

I did not take my usual hunting path by the knoll behind which I had shot three hares on my maiden hunting outing I went by the main shorter one to the left. It leads up to a peak and then descends into the marshy lower side of the forest where I might find wild duck. Besides, there was a greater possibility of shooting partridge or squirrel for first game because of the type of vegetation on the land.

I was walking fast and getting hot. Normally it was a one-hour leisurely trek to the edge of the thick forest behind the suburbs of our part of the town but, in my anxiety, I did it in about forty-five minutes.

The sun, though bright, was barely warm. That was the time when most animals in the forest broke their fast.

The dew would still be on the grass but warm enough for enjoyable eating for herbivores. As they came out for food, the carnivores would be stalking them for their own food and I would be there after both.

I had to stop to catch my breath and regain the calm I would need to shoot with a steady gun. I would do so beside the brook at the entrance into the forest.

I noticed that the gun had become a lot heavier than when I left the house. In fact the weight seemed to increase as I approached the forest.

By the time I got to the slope beside the brook, there was already a deep depression in my left shoulder where the leather strap made contact with my flesh through the shirt.

Now I was sweating profusely even though it was still fairly cool. The hard climb had done it. Thirty yards from the brook of sparkling water, I sat on a mound of soft greenish-brown grass on the exposed top of a black boulder to rest, being careful not to sit on an unsuspecting green snake.

I placed the weapon gingerly on the grass to let it also rest for a while. I dropped the hunting bag beside it. In some way there was something inexplicably tense about that gun.

On the surface it was just an ordinary arrangement of shaped pieces of metal and wood stuck together but inside there was something abnormal. I sensed it.

Below me the brook had overflowed its banks and smoothed the grass on the lower part of the submerged boulder where it spread its clear water.

It was early rainy season but most streams were already full. Further down, the brook left a puddle of crystal-clear, thirst-provoking water on the left and flowed on rightwards towards the marshes.

The whole area had a pleasant coolness. I looked with misgiving at the treacherous damp mosses on the surface of the wetter parts of the dark exterior of the great rock.

A loss of balance on any of these would send a person catapulting involuntarily down to the threatening grass-covered lower part of the stone some eighty yards below.

When I was rested, I picked up the gun to get into action. I broke it, thrust one cartridge into each of its barrels and put on both safety catches. I now took a sprightly step forward.

I was certain that any game that hazarded itself into my way would be in my pot that evening. That obese disease-ridden woman would long for the least bit in vain.

The Mother of Ache would be proud of me when I returned home. She ought to be careful with the big woman really. She would ruin our peaceful marriage by appealing to tradition. She might even end up by killing one or both of us. The woman was cruel and taking life is addictive.

Custom was not going to force her on us. My hunting would produce something to make her feel bad. That would discourage her from any hopes of conjugal life with me. I was sure of success because though the Mother of Ache knew about the trip I had not been with her that night.

CHAPTER THREE

I stood up and was resolutely peering into the shadows of the forest in front of me, with the gun in my left hand, when its weight suddenly became so great that I felt agonizing pain in my left shoulder.

It was as if some powerful hand was trying to use the leather strap to push me down by the shoulder. The strap would either snap or bruise my shoulder if it fell short of making a cut in it.

I took the leather band from my shoulder and held the gun in my right hand. The pain followed my action.

It seemed as if someone of great strength was forcing the fingers of my sweating hand open. I fought back for some time. Soon the pain grew too great for me. I let go.

The gun slipped out of my hand and dropped. My heart sank as I watched it bounce off the hard rock surface a number of times before it hurtled against a tuft of grass rounded by water in the centre of the mighty stone and came to an abrupt stop.

There immediately followed a disturbance in the foliage of trees in front of me. The trees swayed in a spinning wind that was fast gathering strength.

The whirlwind swooped down from them, spinning now like a top and sucked up dead dry leaves and twigs on the grassy slope above me into the atmosphere.

The tornado dived down to the ground on the shrubby

higher side of the forest, picked up every light thing in its way: dry leaves, blades of grass and bone-dry twigs and whisked them into higher heights towards the sky.

I narrowed my eyes into slits in order to stop any dirt from entering them. The spinning air got to me. I would have continued watching its action but it encircled me and intensified its force so much that I fully closed my eyes and instinctively raised my arms to my face.

The embrace of the wind was unpleasantly cold and foul-smelling like brimstone. After a great attempt to carry me away, as it were, the wind stopped and everything around me slowed down and went quiet.

The angry humming of the wind receded into the distant hills. I opened my eyes.

In the silence I heard the gun start its fall again. I saw it clatter weirdly down towards the more grassy lower parts of the mighty stone. There was a final clank and a splash as it dropped into the puddle of clear water and came to a final stop.

The dry leaves and grass that the wind had abandoned in midair floated back down towards the ground in merry slow motion. They began to settle noiselessly around me and I closed my eyes again.

When I opened them all was once more calm. It was as if nothing had happened before.

I was profoundly disturbed. I know how a stick should fall down a slope. The firearm had not fallen that way. Its fall had been animated. The rebound each time was higher than the previous one.

I was not imagining anything. The gun was acting like a young goat, gambolling over the rock exterior provocatively as if a control outside gravity was assisting it in its movements as it was apparently escaping from me.

Now it lay down there as if resting. It had come to a stop just before the whirlwind stopped as if it had been programmed to do so.

I was struck dumb and motionless with my mouth open like a crocodile waiting for flies to enter its trap of wide open jaws. I found it all terrifyingly strange.

I continued staring unblinkingly with my mouth still open and dry. I felt the wetness of cold sweat under the collar of my shirt and in my armpits. My chest was rising and falling violently as I panted. My chest hurt. I had to watch that dangerous thing in the small pool down there.

My eyes were fixed on the weapon which I saw through some kind of weird grayish mist. Of a sudden, it rose out of the shallow water. It thrust itself upwards out of the water on its own. I was definitely not imagining anything.

Water was dripping from the rubber padding at the bottom of its highly polished butt. Then the weapon continued to rise, now purposely slowly and came to a suspended stop in the empty air, not resting on anything.

It hesitated there and then swung over above the dry grass where it hung balanced as if catching its breath and watching me ominously. After a seemingly thoughtful wait, it calculatingly lowered itself onto the grass underfoot.

I could not believe my eyes! It had to be some optical illusion. The spring action of a branch on which the gun had been lying must have thrust it from underneath upwards. It had then slid onto the dry grass above.

That neither accounted for its rising into the air as if lifted by human hands nor its suspension in the air before lowering itself onto the dry grass.

I could not find any satisfactory explanations to the disturbing questions that went through my tormented mind. Now drenched in sweat, I decided to go down there and sort things out for myself.

In a split second the gun rose some three feet off the grassy ground. It remained suspended in midair once more! At first both its barrels pointed into the grass whence it had just risen.

It was not possible! I would carry out my resolve to go down there or go insane. I was beginning to think of the best way to do so when an even stranger part of the spectacle began to unfold.

The firearm quickly swung towards me at the height at which a man would hold a shotgun. I could still not see anything holding it as it further rose to the level of a man's shoulder as in a man's stance when he is preparing to shoot.

The nostrils of the barrels pointed in my direction and rose to the level of my chest, more exactly the level of my heart.

My mouth went dryer. I was quite unable to shut it. I swallowed hard and must have stopped breathing for a few seconds. I tried to clear my throat but felt excruciating pain.

Something gripped the muscles in my neck so hard that they seemed to be on fire. Before my eyes, the two barrels set their sights and their perfectly round nostrils were glaring implacably at me.

I now saw. The gun was taking aim! The proof was its motionlessness and an infinitesimal, almost imperceptible movement of the safety catches to "off" position, followed by a rock steadiness of the entire gun.

The triggers would soon tighten and … I was momentarily paralyzed. I felt as if I was in a straightjacket, unable to move. There was a painful throbbing in my head. My heart was pounding so fast and with such force that I feared one of my   ribs would crack.

I heard myself gasp and a veil floated away from over my

face. My head cleared like the sudden opening of a door out of a dark room into bright daylight. It dawned on me that I was waiting to be killed.

With needles pricking me all over my body, I sprang into action. I kicked forcefully with my legs like a frog does with its hind legs. I was already airborne in a dive towards the brook the instant both triggers moved.

They thrust themselves simultaneously towards the back of the gun. My right shoulder hit the water just before the explosions from the twin barrels.

I was stunned. The gun had shot at me!

All these things happened in a tiny immeasurable amount of time. The resulting thunderous reverberations were terrible. They bounced off hill after hill into infinity.

Inside the forest monkeys cried out in uncommon alarm for over three minutes while some amphibians in the marshes croaked intermittently.

I lay across the brook, making a dam with my body and getting soaked through and through but enjoying being alive. Death had missed me and life was so much sweeter.

If I had not had the foresight to dive away from the shotgun pellets, I would have been a corpse with my precious blood splashed on the grass around like that of any common animal shot to death with a shotgun.

I would have been shot by my own gun. The thought made me sweat the more even though I was lying in cold flowing water.

I remained where I lay for I know not how long, trying to recover from the shock and figure out the bizarre action of a gun, supposedly mine, that had become viciously animated and inimical.

With a great effort, I made myself stand up. I had to accept what had happened – the fact that a gun, on its own, or through the influence of an invisible force or forces unknown, would shoot at its owner.

I was pensive, beaten and humiliated by some enigmatic evil energy. I determined not to stay there moping. I had to do something. I was not just a man. I was one of identical twins and therefore an extraordinary man.

With laden feet I dragged myself to the mound of soft green grass on which I had been resting. It was here that I had stood looking down at the gun below.

The grass had been mowed down and even dug up in places by hot AA shot. I would have been cut in half.

My brown leather hunting bag was mangled and completely destroyed. It had been an expensive bag big enough to take an antelope. It would now serve better as a sieve than the bag for game that it had been.

I had to check around the pond. There might be clues lying there. I gnashed my teeth and skated roughly down to the killer-gun which somehow had once more taken up its original position in the water like the ordinary gun that it was not.

I stood scrutinizing it at my feet with fear mixed with repulsion. It was but a thing – metal and wood fashioned together for killing.

It could not have moved itself. It had to have been moved by some undetectable might since all round me no footprints rewarded my meticulous search.

I thought that by examining the weapon more closely, I might get a clue to what had happened. I picked it up and examine it with narrowed eyes. Everything was as it ought be. There was nothing abnormal about it.

The gun felt much lighter, as light as it had been when I cleaned it in my house early that morning. Evil might have been drained from it to leave it with its normal weight.

With shaking hands, I slung it uncertainly over my shoulder to climb back to the path that would take me back home. The thought of hunting was now tasteless.

After a few unsteady strenuous steps, I realised that the surface of the great stone would be too treacherous to attempt to climb.

I plodded my way back to the pond and took a longer roundabout way to my ruined leather bag. It was near it that I would have been killed. I scooped the soil from within it and searched inside its small compartments.

The two cartridges were still there, untouched. I put them in my left breast pocket. The desire to hunt was now revolting. It might never be rekindled in my lifetime.

Had that gun moved or been moved? Inanimate things do not, as a rule, move of their own accord. Therefore it had been moved. I had made the same conclusion before.

Could Thecla Ado or her brother or both have had something to do with what had happened? I was at a loss to see how.

From what place on earth could the moron or the enormous porpoise, who was passing for my brother's widow, have got such strange power.

It would be more me, the buffalo of the Itung twins, to possess supernatural power, not any of them, the most ordinary of mortals that they were.

Could it have been my brother wielding the weapon with the intention of taking me into his new place of abode since I would not obey him? The attempt on my life came so soon after he had appeared to me in the nightmare. That appearance might have been to forewarn me of his impending action.

CHAPTER FOUR

I got to the outer uninhabited reaches of our quarter at about noon and stopped at the spot where the path split into two. The one left was shorter. It was my usual way and I should not take it to avoid meeting my enemy.

Or I could go the longer way right and enter the compound from the front.

This way also had its problems for it passed by a little square where idle young men of the quarter regularly hung out.

The inquisitive loafers would want to know what game I had brought back home. Finding me with none, they would exchange looks and start laughing at me through irritating comments. What might happen if I lost my temper in my present mood was anybody's guess.

I would rather face Thecla Ado than the mocking scoundrels of the square. I went down the path briskly, anxious to get past my foe. I got to the back of the   compound. If I could only go past without the vixen seeing me!

I entered the compound beside Kang's house. If I had carried a horse on my shoulders, it would have been a lighter weight than the one I was carrying on my mind. I avoided looking at Kang's humble grave at the back.

The perpetually loud and raucous voice of my supposed sister-in-law reached me without her seeing me. She was singing some wild calypso she must have learnt during the long years she had spent wasting my brother's money, our family money, in the United Kingdom.

She had never learnt to talk or sing in a low voice. If she spoke into one's ear, in her idea of a soft voice, one would be temporally deaf. If she shouted, one's hearing would be permanently impaired.

The compound my brother had built for us was possessed of three houses. His was the one to the east, a comfortable modern villa with floors of beautiful shining dark brown tiles, four bedrooms, each with its own toilet, and a spacious living room that was the envy of the director of the populous ballroom dancing school in town.

The back of the villa was where the native house of our parents had been. It was in it that we had been born long before the coming of the hospital in town. Kang had built his house for a large family that he was destined never to have thanks to the capacious female.

To the west was a small house for me. It had two large bedrooms which opened into an oblong living room. The third house to the south had been built for my parents but they had both died – Father ten months before Mother – in their old native house before the construction of their new house was finished.

We buried them in front of their house which we demolished after Mother's burial.

According to modern law, Kang had died intestate. His Amazon of a woman was said to have the right to inherit the whole compound. By customary law, the compound, with everything in it – including the woman, believe it or not – was mine.

That meant that my soi-disant sister-in-law would become my second wife with whom I would beget children in the name of my brother. These children I would bring up with mine to ensure the continuation of our great family in a big way.

The very thought of touching that large woman made my blood run cold. There were better ways of committing suicide than this disgraceful, painful one.

I entered the compound warily. The fragrance of a beautiful expensive perfume struck my nose. It would surely be from Thecla Ado. No other woman in the environs could afford that scent.

She came out to the porch of my brother's house, singing her insipid song with abandon.

The perfume lost its verve.

She greeted me in her most welcoming tone of voice. I did not answer. I was not her playmate. She watched me closely as I went past her. She would next say something unpleasant.

"The Father of Ache," she said through an irritating giggle. "Welcome back from hunting. Don't forget my share of the bush meat you've brought. I too have a mouth to eat meat with, you know?"

I pushed the strap of the gun forward and strode along in fury.

"Your business," I spat out.

"The Father of Ache, I did not kill your brother! We hardly ever disagreed. Hate me as you do for anything else and not for something I didn't do, please."

"Don't tell me! I didn't ask you anything."

"I don't know why you hate me so Fung. Perhaps you think I am ill. Go and see my doctor. You must start doing your duty to me as your wife. And you should give that gun to my brother. Those were Kang's last words to you and you're supposed to obey them."

I went past her at a safe distance. She had the ability to talk for a whole day without stopping. Her last utterance infuriated me.

"Stop that crap!" I growled.

Nothing could stop the lump of fat from finishing what she intended to say. She always had to have the last word in any conversation.

That was what she had learnt in white people's country. She needed Africanization to regain the local hue. Head bowed, I strode on towards my house.

"Look into the centre of the earth if you care," she cried caustically. "But you can still see me, your second wife, and that is what matters. You shall one day have to tell me why you hate me so."

With the corner of my eye, I saw her mighty shape looking curiously at me. I had to say something back to her before continuing my way.

"You always have energy for words," I said. "Go on. Sing as long as you want for all I care."

Her voice broke as she went on. I feared she would burst into tears.

"Don't think it's my wish," she said through a sob she was fighting to suppress. "You think I'd want to marry a man who hates me as much as you do? You're so much like your late brother and yet you do everything to be different as far as I'm concerned."

I waved my right hand over my right ear.

"Go and fall in Lake Awing!" I retorted mercilessly.

She noticed I was carrying nothing but the gun.

"Oh, I'm sorry I didn't know the hunting was so bad today," she said with genuine contrition in her voice.

She should not think that I was softening up.

"Go to hell!" I shouted.

She tried an uncaring, mischievous laugh which did not

touch me.

"I wouldn't fail to beg you if I had to but I'm not going to," she cried. "It's the will of your brother. It's the tradition of your people. I shall keep reminding you of it. You're to give that gun to my brother, your brother-in-law. Your brother said so on his dying bed. I told Alemus to come and see you this evening. Please give him the gun when he comes. I have left your food with the Mother of Ache, my mbanya."

I stopped in mid-stride and half turned round with my head cocked to one side.

"Your what?" I shouted. "Mbanya indeed! You must be mad. There shall never be any such thing."

She clapped and folded her clubs of arms across her ample bosom.

"Mad? Not me," she replied complacently. "The traditions of your tribe must be. Anyway, you know the tradition better than I. You can't push me into ignoble behaviour. I shall never be that kind. If your parents had not died −"

I noticed the neat hairline above her forehead. A comma of silky hair reached down into her right ear. On another woman it would have been exquisite. On this one it was like a mockery of beauty.

"What would they have had to do with it?" I snarled, stopping momentarily while looking in the direction of my house.

Her huge body took a step towards me. I took two quick steps away from her.

"Everything!" she cried. "You'd have had to listen to them."

I continued my way with undue speed.

"Say what you like. I don't care!" I shouted. "Just leave me alone!"

She dropped her arms and spread her hands in frustration.

"I'm not holding you, am I?"

I felt good. I had not weakened in any way. I must keep the hatred of the murderess of my brother alive. She had, however, said a few things that were disturbingly true.

Like the educated woman that she was, she knew what to say to bamboozle a man and have her way. She was not going to have that with me.

If I went on listening to that woman, I would be enraged enough to kill her with my bare hands or with the gun she so much wanted for her brother. Which gun?

The pictures of the events around the great rock went through my mind in review. My throat began to ache with strong emotion. I entered my house boiling like water for cooking fufu corn. I got to my house and slammed the door after me and involuntarily bolted it.

The widow by assertion was regular in her supply of food. It meant she was regular in doctoring the food to finish me off. It meant the pig was continuously eating doctored food.

Pigs have a lot in common with human beings. Therefore if the food was being doctored, it would have long killed the pig. Since the pig had not died, Thecla Ado may not have been doctoring the food. .

So she might not want to kill me. She probably did not dislike me. That was a lie. A fat lie indeed! I was fooling myself into a grave that would be wider and deeper than my brother's.

Tradition required me to give food money to my brother's widow, now my self-styled wife, every market day. My brother had left a fortune for her in the house and people would have me add more?

I would rather die first. Doing so would give her horrible confidence. She would covet all my family property.

There was also a heavy amount of money in Kang's account in the bank. Rumour had it that the corpulent woman had applied for letters of administration from the Probate Office of the High Court of our province. As Kang had died intestate, they intended to give her jurisdiction over his estate, completely ignoring me.

I did not know what the custodians of our golden tradition would say to that. I would wait and see. I was in no hurry. The terminal disease from which the bad woman was suffering would get her for me.

Time was going to take away the river in my way and I would need no bridge to get to the other side.

CHAPTER FIVE

I took a bath with the warm water my wife provided and was thinking of siesta to calm my nerves when the ungainly footsteps of Alemus Ache sounded on my veranda.

His sister must have told him I was back home. He was coming as   defiance. Their internal threat and boast was the readiness to see what I would do when the rightful inheritor himself came for his property. The fellow had chosen that day of all days to come and laugh at me. After all he was a much better hunter.

He could not even wait till evening after people had returned from the farm. The sister had surely sent someone to tell him that I had returned from the forest for he would normally have waited till evening to be sure I was at home from the farm or my tailoring workshop.

I could imagine the lopsided smile on his thick lips. He would definitely be bubbling over with happiness in anticipation of laying his filthy hands on my gun.

He was trying to come into the ownership of a gun with neither right to it nor knowledge of its cost. I felt my fists clench.

I could tell him not to set foot in my house, to get out of my compound altogether. I would shout at him in order to enjoy his humiliation as he retreated. He would feel vindicated by running to his sister to report what I had done.

The fellow took all the time in the world to reach my doorstep where he stopped. He stood there waiting as if he was eavesdropping. As time went by tension was building up in me. I sat very quiet not to let him know that I knew he was there.

A sound from my bedroom made me start. There was scraping on the wall on which I had leaned the gun. Could little Ache have gone in there without my noticing him? If I found him there, I would wring his ears.

I went into the room to check. It was empty. No one had touched the gun for it was against the wall as I – not quite as I had placed it.

There was a strange brightness coming from both its barrels. I peered at them, the strangeness of the appearance making me momentarily distrust my sight.

A certain ominous bright red luminescence that I could not help connecting with vengeful triumph was coming from both barrels. That gun again!

The thought of touching the animated firearm at that moment so scared me that I put both my hands into the pockets of my trousers.

I looked across at the main door for a spell. There came a quick scraping from the direction of the gun. I thought I caught sight of quick movement. It was so fast that I began to doubt both my senses of sight and hearing.

I glanced away and the scraping quickly took place once more. The gun was timing me to play its tricks. It knew what it was doing! It was going to show me who was who in my compound that day. I went to the wall against which it was leaning for a closer look.

At the level of the two nostrils of the gun were several curved lines that had never been there. They made crescent shapes downwards, the last one ending where the nostrils touched the wall. The gun had made those marks by itself!

There was a crimson hue about the lines as if they were tinged with blood. I had not imagined it all. The gun had been scraping the wall in some uncanny demonstration of agitation. It was happy because Alemus had arrived!

It was celebrating the arrival of its true owner, its master. The malicious dastardly thing! It had a mind of its own. So it had known what it was doing when it shot at me that morning. Or, perhaps, some invisible hand had moved it.

I went back into the living room, folded my arms across my chest and stood waiting in deep perturbation. I had never felt so helpless in my life.

I did not know what to do, not even where to look. I felt like a stranger in my own house.

Alemus stood outside the door as if he was planted there. He would not come in. He would not even knock on the door.

He knew I was aware of his presence. After all he was a creditor there.

The mocking smile on his homely face was to irritate me. If he would not come in, let him stay the whole day out there.

Then it occurred to me that I could solve the problem once and for all. Yes, I could do it. I studied the two cartridges on the table in the centre of the room. Why not?

I could. Get the gun and load it with them, take aim at the door as the urchin was coming in and pull both triggers simultaneously when his body blocked the doorway. Boom!

The gun had done it to me. I should better it all by doing it to my enemy. The imp would be cut in two. After that the gun would forever be mine undisturbed by Kang's imitation of a brother-in-law.

I was so distraught that I did not think of the aftermath of such an act.

I contemplated the gun. Then I realised that it would not do. That gun was my antagonist and would rather do it to me.

I might load it and, using occult power, it would twist itself round in my hands and shoot me in the heart. I would have loaded the gun for the taking of my own life.

I suddenly felt hot. Sweat burst from my brow and my palms were damp. That gun was not for me. It was against me.

Since it surely had a will of its own and a mystical force at its disposal, it would be foolhardy for me to attempt to use it against its master.

There was nothing I could do with it. As far as I was concerned, it was a lethal weapon and an unfathomable ally of my enemy.

At last Alemus began to wipe his awkward feet on the rack on the threshold. The handle of the door turned slowly but the door was locked.

The bushman knew nothing of the politeness of knocking. The Mother of Ache had taken the blind off for washing. I could see the rustic grinning like a whale shark through the glass at the upper part of the door.

I went over and turned the key in the lock. He stood there opening his mouth some more before he opened the door and strutted into my living room. I looked indifferently at the expression of unease on his face.

His maddening presence made me breathe so badly that I nearly choked. He left the door wide open. I was sweating profusely all over as I went back to the door and slammed it shut so that he would be reminded of what he should have done.

The fool was going to make me destroy my own door. I returned stiffly to where I had been standing.

To my great annoyance, Alemus continued grinning in the centre of the room. I put great energy into looking daggers at him.

The idiot would not say anything. I looked longingly at the side stool beside me. I could smash his head with it. The desire to do him harm was gnawing at me in my guts like a bundle of squirming round worms.

At that moment all energy abruptly drained from my body. I walked wearily backwards until the back of my legs struck the closest sofa and it moved up to my backside. My knees flexed and I felt myself crash into the chair.

I made out a leering expression on the gun-seeker's face. He was rubbing his hands together contentedly and moving his head from side to side like some monkeys do when enjoying a meal.

I did not ask him to sit down since I had not invited him to my house. He put his hand over his mouth and coughed.

I heard violent scraping from the gun inside my room. That animated thing was at its mischievous work once more. What would these people not make me experience?

I stood up and the sofa creaked. The scraping stopped. The thief of a gun was hypersensitive. It knew what it was doing all right. It was showing me who its master was by action and yet trying to be stealthy about it.

I looked at my antagonist to find out whether he was aware of anything strange. He did not seem to be but he could be putting on an act. He might not want me to know that he knew about his ally's signals from my room.

He was dressed in cheap mourning as if it was his brother who had died. Well, he would have to add "-in-law" after "brother" if that would make any difference.

I recognised the Salamander boots he was wearing. They had been my late brother's. His sister had given them to him without letting my brother's body settle down in its grave. She was distributing his property without consulting me.

I had been right to have disapproved of their fake marriage from the very beginning. To me it had never taken place. That court show the creature had got my brother to do in the United Kingdom amounted to nothing.

She had no right to give away anything of my brother's without my express permission. Who did she think she was anyway? An Itung? I could order her brother to take them off and go back home barefooted. Instead of putting my thoughts into action, I stared at the fellow.

He came to where I was sitting and held out his hand. I was listening for more scraping from the gun. I ignored his appendage, stood up hurriedly and went towards my room. I stopped at the door to listen.

Part of my attention was on my unwelcome visitor. Many people do not know their place in society. The phony marriage of my brother to his sister did not place him on the same rung of the social ladder like us.

Yet, somewhere deep down in this commoner's being, he must have been thinking that he was more than my equal.

I did not know what I was going to do. I had only become painfully aware that the safety of my life lay in giving the gun away. The thing had shown in more than one way that it did not like me. Why should I take it by force?

CHAPTER SIX

I entered my room once more and found that the gun had further scratched off a wide crescent shape of paint and plaster from the wall. I picked it up, fighting the urge to slam it against the wall and break it.

As I was going back into the living room, gun in hand, the intruder was standing with arms akimbo and smiling up at the ceiling, waiting to lay his stumpy, gnarled fingers on my gun.

He had installed some magic in that gun. I could have died from the rage that was shaking my body. The moron was owner of my property! I could die from the humiliation.

The weapon was as light as a feather. I moved up to Alemus and thrust it forward, almost jabbing the miscreant's chest with it as I intentionally held it out the wrong way, with the barrels pointing at the hateful beating heart within his skeletal chest.

He stepped back and gently pushed the firearm from his chest, thinking that I was ignorant of the correct way of giving a gun to a person.

I could have leapt on him there and then and strangled him with my bare hands or beaten his head into bloody pulp with the gun.

I hated him with a passion I had never thought I possessed. He was at the centre and height of their meddling in my family affairs.

"That's not the right way to give a gun to a person, Big

Brother," he croaked through his cigarette-smoke-stained teeth.

I wondered whom the impish clown was calling 'Big Brother'.

"Take the damn thing!" I said through gnashed teeth. "Take those two cartridges on the table too. And get out!"

I was wasting my time. My shout did not disturb him in the least.

Bowed low, he stretched out both arms and took the gun reverently in them. A few flashes of green ran down the barrels. I was definitely not imagining anything. I saw everything with my own eyes.

Alemus looked at me in surprise. His mouth hung open as if to let flies enter. He passed his tongue over his scorched thick lips. I was deeply pained by what Kang was making me go through.

"So-so it's true," the caricature of a man stammered, "what Sister said. He left me the gun. Your brother was such a good man."

I looked at him, putting all the animosity I could muster into the look. I was hot. My body was shaking. Alemus remained calm. He did not discern anything disagreeable in my expression.

The little animal was void of brains. He had eyes that saw without registering anything in his brain. Yet he would be owner of the gun.

I was infuriated by the maddening waste of time but fought the feeling for I would only hurt myself with any foolish action.

I would have loved to say something really nasty to the apathetic ruffian if he would understand but I went dumb and not a word came out of my mouth. I felt a lump in my throat and my fists clench and unclench of their own accord.

"I'm sorry if I've disturbed you in any way," the object of

my loathing went on. "I shall have to come back here to give you the first game I shoot with this gun that you people have been so kind to give me."

I remained silent and he mistook this for listening. He did not know I was fighting the impulse to turn my hatred into violent physical action.

I strode to the door, yanked it open and stood waiting, with my eyes half closed in cold rage, for him to get out. He picked up the two cartridges on the table and walked out noiselessly without looking at me.

I shut the door with a slight bang, dragged myself back to one of my sofas and began to rack my brains on what course of action to follow.

After some fifteen minutes of foot-stamping, teeth-gnashing, moping and mental turmoil, a great calm descended on me. The damn thing had tried to kill me. Let it go! Let it get out of my life!

Alemus had not taken the sheath of the gun for it lay on the floor beside the chair at the door into my room. I picked it up, went to the main door and called to him as he was about to put his hand on the doorknob of the villa wherein his sister lived.

He ran to my door but I did not give him a chance to meet me there. I threw the sheath on the ground and shut the door before he got there. The idiot!

I sat down and took time to think. I was wrong to have disobeyed Kang's instructions. Moreover it was only right and just to respect the last words of a dead man especially if he had been one's identical twin brother.

'Let the will of your brother be done.' said a tiny little voice somewhere in my head. No matter their provenance little voices did not know much. This one thought I had obeyed it when I gave the gun to Alemus.

My little voice did not know the importance of the gun. It only knew how to interrupt my judgment in favour of huge Thecla Ado's brother. I had given the gun away to save my life, not in obedience of my brother.

The voice of my cowardly conscience told me that my brother had bought the gun and had the right to decide who would own it after his death. His spirit might have been what had animated the firearm in its attempt to kill me.

I doubted it very much for the deceased part of a person may not try to kill the living one. Anyway, I could not be certain since I had never died even though my other half had.

I tried to relax. The two of us, identical twins, may have been one but I alone was still alive and therefore could think better. Kang was a spirit. Did spirits think at all? This one ought to think in its identical twin brother's favour.

The weapon should have been mine. The issue of ownership of the gun had become my monomania. As I had given it away, it was time I got it out of my system.

I had to fight against the vacuum created by the absence of the gun. Fool that I had become, I needed to pinch myself for common sense to come back into my brain. My foes had defeated me in the fight for the firearm. They would want me to feel their victory every time we met.

I was now reduced to a little mongrel whimpering in its kernel to amuse any passerby. The pain of defeat is indeed great.

In my despair I wished I were dead. Then I thought of how my demise would be a windfall for my enemies and determined to live on, if for nothing else but being in their way.

I wondered where, on dying, I would have left my wife and son and realised that my life was a lot more than the possession of the gun.

Thecla Ado was enjoying doubly in that her brother had

the gun and she was living in my brother's villa as hers.

She must be very brave to live in that big house by herself. Both my parents were buried behind the house which was in front of where their own native house had been.

Her husband was buried there also. The three graves on the other side of the back wall of her bedroom did not worry her at night. Perhaps the overweight woman did not have enough imagination to be afraid.

If it was I who had died, the Mother of Ache would not have the courage to live in our house all alone.

Even if she was a murderess, there obviously was something special about my brother's wife. The mistake she had made was to open her mouth to talk about the gun.

I could have decided to lend it to her brother each time he wanted to go hunting and instructed him to bring it back immediately afterwards.

I would let him use the gun to supply me bush meat but not let him own it. His using it in that manner would have been respecting my brother's instructions halfway because we were two halves of one. That should have satisfied him in his grave.

I felt the chair below me. There was food in two bowls on the dining table. I had not noticed the Mother of Ache putting it there. I had not the least appetite. I went into my room and lay down in bed.

The atmosphere was void of charge. There was nothing fearsome about the lines that had been scratched on the wall by the evil gun. The crimson was gone from them. The source of my torture was gone.

I felt drowsiness grab me. I was going to be able to truly rest. I fell into a deep sleep.

CHAPTER SEVEN

Two days after taking possession of the gun, Alemus, for it had to be him from the way he shuffled down the veranda of my house, arrived at my front door at 5.30 a.m. He knocked on the door in his timid clumsy way.

It was a rather cold misty morning of a country Sunday, a day when people did not go to the farm. I usually lazed around till early in the afternoon and would attend traditional marriage parties and crydies to which I had been invited.

I was furious at this intrusion on my day's programme and came out of my room belligerently. Was his taking of the gun not enough? Did he have to further rub in my defeat? He thought it was now his right to come barging into my house so early in the morning. I would have it out with him. This would be the first and the last time.

A vicious shout was at the tip of my tongue when I thought the better of it and, out of curiosity mixed with fear that he might be the bearer of bad news, went to the front door to find out what he wanted.

My fury had ebbed into displeasure as I switched on the security light outside so as to see before I was seen.

It was Alemus alright. He stood revealed with some heavy burden across his shoulders. I took a step closer and looked through the pane of the door.

The fellow's load was in his dirty brown hunting jute bag

with blood stains on most of its lower half.

I looked closer still and saw the hooves of a gigantic brown antelope protruding from the mouth of the bag. The man must be as strong as an ox to bear such weight and not be bent over.

I unlocked and opened the door wide to let him enter the house. He crouched low and squeezed through the doorway, breathing heavily, and proudly threw the bloody brown bag with a heavy thud on the floor.

He then gripped the bag, loosened the rope from the mouth and pulled it away from the carcass of the quadruped. Lumps of jellylike gore dropped on the multicoloured linoleum.

My wife surprised me with a loud exclamation behind me. Alemus was watching me guardedly under the fluorescent light bulb. His lips were stretched in his usual easy grin.

He must have spent the whole night in the forest, hunting with the help of the big electric torch that hung from his neck by a rubber band. All alone in the forest at night! It took a real man to do that kind of thing.

I had to admit grudgingly to myself that it was bravery far beyond my capacity. I was incapable of doing such a thing. And then with that gun – I would not have come back home alive.

Comfortable light of an indescribable pleasant colour was emanating from the gun hanging from the hunter's shoulder. I did not know whether the light was meant solely for my eyes or other people could see it also. Whatever the situation, there was no enmity about it.

Alemus took the gun down and laid it on the antelope's body. I was tense and apprehensive. Here was a man returning me good for all the evil I had thought and done him and his sister.

This would have been a good opportunity, were it somebody else, were it even me, to bring up the matter of antipathy and seek reparation. There was no such thing on Alemus's honest mind. His countenance showed only tiredness, happiness and satisfaction.

He took a cartridge from his left trouser pocket and held it up for me to see. Then carefully put it back.

"The one left of your two," he said drowsily. "I'll try for some other thing in a fortnight. I have to go to the house for a little rest and to attend to some business."

I stepped forward to have a better look at the dead antelope whose blood trickled from the pink inside of its nostrils and was spreading on the floor.

It was so much meat, surely over sixty kilogrammes, but he did not seem interested in taking the least thing for himself. Perhaps he would later.

I kept marvelling at what the brother of Thecla Ado had done. I could not have done it. Bravery seemed to run in their family for his sister too was brave in her own way. She lived all alone in her late husband's big house.

She had to be a woman apart because very few women in our community could do that. I had to admit, despite myself, that there was some microscopic good in her.

I kept staring at the carcass. Alemus was looking at me blandly. He did not take his eyes off my face as he took a few steps away from the carcass and came hesitantly towards me. I did not retreat.

He kept on coming forward. He got so close that our bellies were virtually touching. His look did not waver. I felt neither discomfort nor revulsion.

No odour of cigarette smoke emanated from his body. The teeth in his half open mouth were clean, white and even. He certainly did not smoke. I had credited him all along with a thing he was not guilty of.

He let the brown bag drop beside the animal on the floor and raised his arms uncertainly as if he was confused about the action he wanted to take.

A lump the size of an orange suddenly blocked my throat. I swallowed and before I knew what was happening, my arms too had risen and the hunter and I were locked in a powerful embrace.

Then tears of remorse burst from my eyes. They flowed abundantly and wet his left cheek and the grime-coated collar of his dark green hunting shirt.

"Take it easy brother," he whispered in a raucous voice. "Your brother was such a good man. An excellent man. He is in heaven. You too are a wonderful man."

I wanted to tell him that I was not good. I wanted to start reciting a litany of wrongs I had done him in thought, word and action and apologize for everything but only a lame utterance escaped my mouth.

"What can I say?" I heard myself say.

He continued talking as if he had not heard me.

"You first of all let me name your son. The other day you gave me the gun as your brother had said. Your brother told me that with the gun I was never to let you, the Mother of Ache, that is my mother, and Thecla ever lack meat. I have always loved you, you know?"

The last words sparked off a pain in my chest. The gun going to him was for my good! Also he had always loved me. He had just told me as much with his own mouth. I was sobbing uncontrollably now.

I remembered the smoked game, ripe plantains or palm wine he used to give me once in a while. At that time he used to shoot game with his own gun, a flintlock

The brothers-in-law I knew took from their sisters'

husbands. They did not give. Alemus was made of uncommon stuff.

I had taken all that for granted and would not see his love. I was such a heel. He had no evil in his heart. It was I who did. I was totally unable to stop sobbing.

My hitherto neglected brother-in-law tightened his arms round me. His spare body had surprising strength. I felt him shaking with emotion.

I had been such an unfair judge to both sister and brother. His own tears dropped on my left shoulder. They were warm with compassion.

My wife, who had been sniffing behind me, began to cry in earnest in the same timbre of voice as when Kang died. She stepped forward, threw herself on both of us and tried to tie our bodies together with her weak effeminate arms.

For what seemed like an eternity, we stood together in a funny threesome, until I gently pushed Alemus Ache and my wife away to contemplate the game at our feet some more.

I did not try to say anything. It was too hard. Alemus would never know how much I had hated him for no reason at all, good or bad. Thecla Ado's brother was such a wonderful, generous loving man.

Even if his sister did not ever fully become my wife, he would be my brother-in-law. I had just accepted him in my heart. It was in conformity with the dictates of our tradition.

The children that his sister would beget with any man or other men would be mine. I would bring them up as mine and they would bear my family name like my own children. They would be his blood - his nephews and nieces. We were linked together for life. I was so proud to think so.

Kang had been more than the wonderful brother I thought he was. Before going to the grave, he had planned a comfortable life for me. The gun would ensure that. It was his prerogative as my elder brother, yes, elder brother. How would I apologize to a man I could only be privileged to see in spontaneous dreams?

Buffaloes are physically so powerful but have small brains. I had always prided myself with being a very big one. Where had it taken me?

I was glad Alemus would never know the truth. He would never know the extent of my injustice. I had gone as far as toying with the idea of shooting him with the gun.

I wondered whether knowing the truth would have made any difference to him. He was void of any negative feelings. His sister would most probably be like him. Not even depriving him of the gun would have changed him.

The trouble-maker lay across the antelope, seemingly content, seeming to know that it now belonged to its rightful owner. Kang's spirit had unquestionably been in that gun the day it tried to shoot me.

Since I had been unbending, he wanted me to be in the same element like him so that we could sort things out. And how would that have left our people back here? That was a thing he might have forgotten in his anger.

Alemus Ache turned to me, smiling through the tears that still hung in his eyes. I was surprised to discover that he was possessed of good looks and great poise.

I was now breathing with so much ease in his presence. His love was healing me. My heart glowed with affection for this man of high morality. Where had I kept my eyes all those years?

"My father, I must be going," he said, wiping his eyes with the back of his hands as he strode towards the door. "I must have a bath and attend to some business. I'll be back later to help you take care of the meat."

I watched his powerful back as he strode to the door and

placed his hand on the knob.

"You can't do that!" I cried. "You're leaving your gun behind."

He turned round and wagged his right forefinger at me. It was a loving filial warning. I liked it.

"Wrong," he said. "It isn't my gun alone. It's our gun over which you have priority. Even when a son buys a gun, it is first his father's for had the father had him aborted he would never have lived to do anything. Don't you ever forget that, my dear father."

"What a stubborn son you are!" I cried in mellow jest. "I'll pull your ears one of these days."

"I'll only submit to it. It's your right, Papa," he said. "I have nothing to say against it."

He closed the door softly after him, chuckling as he took quick steps out of my house. I managed to swallow the lump that had come back to my throat.

CHAPTER EIGHT

It was a few minutes after six and fairly clear outside. I went to the window to watch him through the windowpane. It was obvious where he was going. He strode up the slope towards my late brother's house with a sprightly step, despite having spent a whole night out roaming the forest without sleeping, and knocked on the sister's door.

In a moment his sister opened it. It was as if she had been waiting for him. She was in a flowing nightwear of lilac colour. She was kind of different and I kept looking in her direction until I felt the Mother of Ache's eyes on my back.

I should have turned round but wondered why I should. I kept looking at the duo up there as if I was unaware of my wife's quizzical look. Sister and brother talked for a while. Then the sister wiped her eyes with the sleeve of her dress.

My heart shrank within me. She was in tears. Her misery must be connected with me in one way or the other. I did not know whether to enjoy her sadness or share in it.

The brother rubbed the back of her head affectionately, pulled her to his chest, patted her on the back and left rather hastily. Thecla stood there looking towards my house.

"So much love between them," the Mother of Ache said at my elbow.

I turned round with a feigned start, pretending that I was not aware that she had been there. She caught her breath and might have been expecting me to burst into anger. She had said too much to the lost cause that I was. I would surprise her.

"Yes," said I evenly. "It's true."

Disbelief showed on my wife's face. She said no more on the matter but pointed at the antelope.

"We'd better taken the animal outside." she said. "More blood is oozing from the nostrils and making a mess on the floor. You'll have to start work on it before her brother comes back."

"That's right."

We managed to half carry and half drag the animal onto the slab beside the water tap in the yard. Slight Alemus had carried it all alone from the distant forest!

I did not know how soon I would stop discovering things that surprised me about my son's namesake.

I immediately began to work on the meat as best I could. It was much more than a big goat and was still warm inside. I worked without any interruption for little Ache had already gone out to play.

He had taken a look at the game after getting out of bed and did not like the sight of the gore. He went to our neighbour's down the road to play football with his friends.

Only half my mind was on what I was doing. The other half was on Thecla Ado. She too could feel. She too could cry. She too could love. And I kept asking myself "Why not".

Though the Mother of Ache was busy in the kitchen, I kept summoning her to assist me with the work. As I worked with mental distraction, I touched my left hand painfully a number of times with the sharp knife I was using.

After that I worked with more concentration. I put all the innards in a big basin for washing and left the rest of the carcass for Alemus, the specialist.

Alemus? Hm. A miracle man! Thinking of him had drained all tension from my body. Drugs prescribed by a physician could not have done better. So his sister was capable of softness and love. She could be less than a common opportunist and gold digger.

There could be a great difference between the real Thecla Ado and the one I had created in my imagination. Some little light seemed to be showing up at the end of the long tunnel. A mighty lot of things might have existed only in my mind all these years.

That was the possible hurting truth with which I might have to contend for the rest of my life. I felt uneasy. It might have been better for the truth to continue to be the lie in my head.

I washed the entrails thoroughly and weaved the intestines into short lengths of slimy rope for cooking. Then with the clumsy help of little Ache who had had enough of his games at the neighbour's and come back home, I cut the liver, the spleen, the kidneys and stomach into easily cooked pieces.

All these I dumped in the Mother of Ache's big twenty-litre aluminium pot and placed it over the fire to cook on the makeshift fireplace I had made in the yard. My wife would take care of the details until it was ready. I needed a little rest and great reflection.

I dragged my feet into my living room and sat down at the dining-table with my elbows on it. I was suffering from a curative shock that was permeating my being slowly towards the core. A dark cloud was gradually becoming a fog that would finally clear and permit me to see.

As far as Thecla Ado went, I was in a dark room with a tiny aperture through which I could peep at the bright world outside. The little hole was increasing all the time, enabling me to see more and more of the world. It would finally open wide for me to see all that was outside.

I perceived the situation in another way. The ugly duckling was becoming a swan under my very eyes. Thecla had always been a gold digger with a mind ever calculating for profit, incapable of love for anyone but herself. The veneer I had given her was peeling off.

The cover of the large aluminium pot fell from my wife's hands onto some stones in the yard with a deafening clatter. I took my elbows off the table with a start but I did not make any comment about it as I normally would have done.

A great happening was at my doorstep but I could not tell whether it would be for me or against me. I went outside for a drink of water for the work on the meat had made my throat dry. Then I grabbed my axe and split wood for the Mother of Ache with unnecessary energy.

I was depressed. He still had a mighty lot to say. He would never finish and leave. He continued to talk.

"One important thing more" he took up his talk again. "Talk to Mrs. Ngubett when she comes to see you this afternoon. Console her. Death is death no matter its manner. There is no good one. No bad one. I will now tell you an important part of the story."

I nearly collapsed from sheer frustration which I would not show. The fellow was going to say something more to take up some more of my precious time. My patience would not last forever.

"What is it now, Pa?" It was hard for me to keep impatience out of my voice.

"This is how I think it all happened. Young Ngubett killed two people and yet he did not kill anyone. Don't laugh. It is not a laughing matter. He loved that artificially light-skinned woman to a finish.

"That did not stop her from continuing to have men out-side. Habits die hard. When you move a dog from a place, it is only the place you have changed, not the dog. It remains the dog of old."

I grudgingly saw what he meant.

"The woman went on chasing trousers after marriage. She did not spare her husband's best friend who was more of a brother. Before marriage she had spoilt her womb with her bad behaviour."

"Am I to write that too?"

"Have it your way now. Keep it all in your head and fix it after I have left."

"Okay. Pa."

"There was this old white man with a strong cough whose mistress she had been for many years. He was the expatriate agric. officer for Ubea. When she got the illness from him, she coughed blood and became as thin as this little finger of mine.

"We thought she would die. Dr. Ngan, her father's best friend did wonders for her. Her father's money saved her life. She got well in a way, a way to be a trap to anyone who struck her. I'm sure that's what happened for her to die. She provoked young Ngubett into striking her and he carried ill luck that paved the way to his grave.

"We had all thought she would never marry. Now, out of the blues came young inexperienced Ngubett, easy fish for the old girl. He was employed in the same office in which she worked. She went to work on him and the boy's head spun like a top.

"She caught him like a cat catches a mouse. He went straight for marriage. Her father took a fortune for her bride-price and hurried things up for them to wed before the boy could find out the truth."

My fingers were weary for the work was taking too long.

"So they got married. He caught her in infidelity and killed her?" I asked, hoping to bring the story abruptly to an end.

"Not so fast," the witchdoctor replied. "The girl had hot blood that could not be cooled in a day, a week or even a month of married life. At first she seemed happy and satisfied to have married such a handsome intelligent young man, so much younger than her.

"Soon the force of her previous life descended on her and she went back to her old ways and former male friends. I swear to God that no son of mine shall ever marry a rich man's daughter!"

I wondered why the old boy was telling me his version of the story when the original one was in the exercise books in front of me.

He ought to let me get it directly from the author. I was not going to publish the story twice over. I stifled a yawn and showed him listening interest on my face.

"You have a good reason," I mumbled.

"Did the marriage last?" the witchdoctor continued with a rhetorical question. "Where? It ended in two deaths – that of the woman and her old bank manager boyfriend.

"How could death result from a weak blow to the woman's chest? Dr. Ngan carried out a post mortem on her body but no word was ever heard of it. Man, it's time for me to go back to my job site."

He stood up suddenly with his cap in hand? I put my pen down and stood up too. He straightened his stiff, starched uniform and marched to the door the handle of which he grabbed in his big right hand.

I followed him to the door. He yanked it open and held out his hand. Mine completely disappeared in the shovel. I was glad he did not squeeze as I might have obtained multiple fractures.

"Thank you very much, Pa," I said with a bow over his hand.

"Whatever for?"

"The work on my head and the business you've brought me."

"Don't mention. It's been a pleasure. Bye."

"Bye, Sir."

He strode onto the landing with his size 14 boots and unintentionally slammed the door. He thought nothing of it and continued his way.

I was happy to be out of my hangover. The old witchdoctor's unending talk though boring, was nothing juxtaposed with my headache.

I now understood why some of the members of my njange group were great customers to witchdoctors. Mine was one with a difference for he worked gratis. I went back to my swivel chair.

CHAPTER NINE

Alemus Ache, my son and brother-in-law-to-be returned late in the afternoon to help me finish work on the meat as he had promised.

He alighted from the old rusty bicycle he used once in a while and took out a blue plastic five-litre container of palm wine from a raffia bag and, with a bow, gave it to me. I nodded my gratitude and took the container into my living room where I put it on the cold floor near the cupboard.

He had foreseen what we would need after the meal that was cooking. I went back outside and we sat side by side on the old bamboo bench in the yard.

He told me about his hunting experiences. He loved night hunting with a torch. I told him I was scared of it. He said it was cheap because you kind of cheated the animal.

It was perplexed by the abnormal small moving moon and, while it was staring at it, you shot it between the eyes which reflected the light of the torch on your forehead. I told him about my childhood experiences in hunting.

The Mother of Ache came out of the kitchen and shouted at us. Were we going to spend the whole afternoon talking about animals we had shot when there were raw parts of one in hand waiting to be prepared for cooking and perhaps smoking?

We both stood up guiltily and started to work on the antelope. It was fun being with Alemus. He wielded my butcher's knife like a surgeon. Asking me to hold this or that part of the carcass as need be, he skinned it like one would take off the shirt from an adolescent's body.

He cut the meat neatly into its natural parts. I already visualized a hind leg going to his sister as a gift, a kind of peace offering.

As he was straightening up from the trays in which he had been putting the meat, his sister intentionally slammed the door of the villa and began to come down towards my house with rather heavy steps.

By this time the entrails had been cooking as pepper soup for close to an hour. Thecla came towards us, making an effort to walk with a lively girlish gait. I knew how much courage it took for her to come to my house after our exchange of the other day.

Her brother's presence had spurred her on. I dared look straight at her when she was near. There was something extremely feminine about her. She was not just any woman.

A light breeze rose and blew her dress between her legs and upwards above her knees. She looked surreptitiously in our direction, caught the dress and pushed it down below her knees once more.

It was a simple feminine act but it impressed me deeply as moral and upright. That could not be her. She was behaving out of character. Decency had nothing to do with her.

Something heavy seemed to drop from inside me. My body was no longer heavy with hard feelings. The warmth of Thecla's personality was affecting me.

She wore a pink close-fitting dress that showed off the copper of her skin and the contours of her body. She was so much smaller than I had always thought. Her feet were small, shapely and feminine and her toenails well manicured. I was already going too far with my examination of the poor girl.

She came on towards my house with uncertainty that disturbed me. She was afraid of me – this woman I had thought was so sure of herself, who would not bat an eye at the sight of a poisonous snake.

I suddenly felt wicked and dirty in front of the clean helplessness of the young woman. I had wasted so many years of animosity for nothing. She was harmless. She was lively. She was friendly.

I realised that I was staring at her. Her brother and the Mother of Ache were watching me. I had been holding a hind leg of the meat aimlessly instead of putting it on the tray with the rest of the other parts. As she drew nearer, I felt my face getting warm.

The fact that I was happy she was coming towards me, bewildered me. I looked away after I had put down the leg of meat and tried to bring all my attention back to the job at hand.

I did not want to talk to her for fear that she might stumble and fall or that I might make a foolish move or say something stupid.

With that broad waist, that full bust, the totality of that build and the desirability I was discovering, she had to be full of babies.

Yet she had not given birth to any. She could not be evil, my former impression could not have been correct. There had to be a reason why the children had not come.

Surely her parents had been satisfied with the lavish brideprice we had given them. They had no reason to block her womb with witchcraft. No, they had not bewitched her, their only girl child.

It was just possible that there had been something wrong somewhere outside her. This girl was wholesome. She was far from lead glittering like gold. She was pure gold itself. I could see that too well now. It hurt.

I remembered with a shudder the day I had shouted at the Mother of Ache for telling me that Thecla was a very nice woman. She had said I only needed to really know her.

I had told her never to talk to me about that horrible woman anymore. She could go ahead and know how nice she was by herself. I did not want to be involved.

She had obeyed me but I could see that she would have loved to convince me to care for Thecla. Things were beginning to go her way. She would be happy with the idea of not just a mbanya but one that was Thecla Ado.

It was possible for me to give her that happiness, if – I was terrified at the idea of Thecla jilting me – Thecla would accept me.

She stepped onto my veranda in discomfiture because of our attention, neither knowing in what direction to look nor what foot to step on first. She might still stumble and fall at any moment even though I was not looking directly at her.

If she did, it would hurt me profoundly. I would feel some-how responsible for it. I gnashed my teeth with self-reproach and fixed my look on her brother's active hands.

Since her husband's death – I could now bear the idea of her having been Kang's wife – it was the third time she was coming to my house, aware that I was in. Their house was only some fifty yards from mine.

She was scared of meeting the enemy in his territory and would come either when I had gone out or was busy at the back of the house. I had not gone to her house since the end of the mourning.

My wife went there practically everyday. I had no right to scold her for that. Dragging her feet along the veranda, Thecla looked around her as if she had never set foot in my yard. Her confusion was total.

CHAPTER TEN

Thecla caught sight of her brother sitting by my side and her big eyes widened to two times their normal size. For the first time I noticed that they were a soft clear light brown.

Her look was so naturally soft that it would be impossible for her to work up a hard look. Her perfume reached me long before she did. Unlike the day of my foul-tongued exchange with her, I inhaled it with pleasure. Thinking can make a lot of good things bad.

Here was a young woman I had classified with those in need of home training. Here was my witch. Here was the childless murderess of my brother, the same one the merciless occult of our tribe had spared and the women's group had treated with uncommon leniency.

Here was the gold digging woman who had made my brother spend all his money on her both in the United Kingdom and back here at home. Here was the show-off – the litany was long and well spiced.

She had been proven innocent of murder and infidelity by the trusted institutions of my tribe. It was only I who kept on holding her guilty in my twisted mind.

I awoke from my reverie when Alemus nudged me with his knee to signal his sister's arrival – as if I had not noticed. He was tense.

I saw the glimmer of tears in her eyes. She was distressed

but did not lack courage. She came forward. Her nice scent grew stronger as she drew nearer. I feared I would faint from its bewitching sweet power.

Alemus and the Mother of Ache were making no secret of their watching me. I had got to a point beyond caring. They were free to watch me watch Thecla.

She stopped about two yards from my right side and curtsied, looking intently at her brother to avoid seeing the usual hatred in my countenance. Here was the woman to whom I had given all the evil qualities in the world.

If I had been less apprehensive, I would have slapped myself there and then. Perhaps I would have had some relief from the pain of my remorse.

"Good afternoon the Father of Ache," she greeted with downcast eyes and misgiving in her voice. "Good afternoon Alemus."

Her brother put down the butcher's knife, stood up with arms akimbo.

"Good afternoon Sister Thecla," he replied.

I did not answer her greeting at once. The fragrance that emanated from her enveloped me. I tried to understand myself better but I was so distracted that I looked lingeringly from her smooth feet to her shapely legs, from her rounded waist to her full bust.

I made our eyes meet. It was the first time in our lives that our eyes ever locked. They stayed that way for a few seconds. A lot of warm communication took place.

Surprise showed on her face at last. Then she looked away. The sadness in her expression distressed me the more. It struck me forcefully that she had never done me any wrong. I could not remember even an attempt at a hard look or frown in my direction at any time. Yet I had always made myself hate her so intensely.

"Good afternoon, Thecla," I replied too casually for the situation.

Thecla caught her breath in more surprise. I did not remember ever having called her by any name at all, not to talk of her Christian name. I had always talked to her with a certain inflection of heavy resentment. I was amazed at my own act.

Her brother showed no proof of having noticed anything unusual. My wife had. The way she hung her head, with a little shrewd smile at the corner of her mouth, showed me what was going on in her head.

Having recovered from the shock, Thecla began to nod on and on like a red male lizard on a rock. When the Mother of Ache came out of the kitchen and opened the large aluminium pot in the centre of the yard, she went to it to see what was going on.

I had been wrong to think that she was losing weight. She was as she had always truly been which was much different from what I had blindly imagined all along.

For the first time in my life, I was truly taking notice of her. I thought I liked her the way she was. Fat women were not my brand but she was not fat.

She was more like a little more than medium and was gifted with radiant beauty that I had refused to see before. I bent down to take care of the fire which was burning well.

She avoided looking at me although it was clear that her whole attention was on me. A warm timid smile spread on her soft lips.

This could definitely not be a sudden change on her side. It was on mine. For me it was like waking up from sleep in a body I had been unconsciously longing for.

I gazed into her big tender light brown eyes and her arms

sagged at her sides. It was such a submissive feminine gesture. It would have pleased me had I not seen a measure of understandable fear in it. I wondered again whether this was the same woman I had known.

I could not find the arrogant aggressive boldness I had often imagined I sensed all those years. She was so attractive in her vulnerability.

I could not take my eyes off her body. A force was sucking me towards her and I had to take things easy and be careful or I would lose her by some inappropriate act or word.

Of a sudden disconcerting trepidation swooped down on me. I was terrified of the asking side on which I had fallen. I had all along been on the rejection side.

If I asked and was not given, if she jilted me, I would be a very sad person indeed and the object of ridicule, first to myself, and then the town over.

That would be the least of my worries. The biggest would be looking at myself in the mirror and seeing in retrospect the fool and mean fellow I had been. I would not be able to come to terms with a sorry image that was likely to haunt me for the rest of my life.

Alemus would never know the extent to which I had mistreated his loving sister. The Mother of Ache was not unaware but she was not the woman to go running her mouth about such negative things.

In the present circumstances I should be very careful indeed. I should take one well considered step after the other.

Thecla's mouth remained half open for a short while. I stared at the gap in the upper incisors and took in a quick breath. That kind of opening in a woman's dental formula was always my undoing. I could not fight it. It was the reason for which I had married the Mother of Ache.

Thecla's was neat, being neither big nor small. All those years I had missed enjoying this comely trait even on my brother's behalf. It would have long been mine if I would have it. And I had been violently unwilling. Her humility squeezed my heart to actual physical pain.

Thecla put her manicured right hand over her mouth. Then turned it round and put the back against her lips.

"Tell me," she ordered, "who it is that has finally brought peace and friendliness to this compound?"

"My son, Ache" the Mother of Ache said, pointing towards the bamboo bench on which Alemus and I were sitting, "and our husband I believe."

I shook my head energetically, looking at her straight in the eye. All three of them were quiet.

"It wasn't any of us," I told them.

"Who then was it?" the two women, my two wives, asked in unison.

I pointed at the gun which was leaning indifferently on the wall of the kitchen.

"The gun. Alemus's gun," I said.

Alemus sprang from the bamboo bench, overbalancing it and nearly throwing me down. I quickly pushed the seat down and shifted my backside towards the middle.

Alemus took a step towards me but relaxed when he saw that I had come to no harm.

Thecla stared at her brother and me for a while.

"So that's how it is," she said at last. "Father and son and their gun. Hm. The lucky of the earth."

I tried to play the man.

"Thecla, shut up!" I heard myself say without vim.

It was the second time I was calling her by her Christian name. It was so palatable but I feared to be taken for a fake.

"Wives should not put their mouths in issues that concern father and son, should they, Ache?" I asked looking up at Alemus

Alemus bettered the situation.

"Not at all, Papa," he said, beaming from ear to ear.

Thecla ululated, leapt two clear feet off the ground and danced round the pot over the fire like a twelve-year-old girl.

All of a sudden she stopped dancing and stared at me.

"I'm not sure, I'm not sure I understand," she cried in confusion. "You've never said a kind word to me."

"Meaning?" I asked her.

"You've never ever said a nice thing to me," she answered.

"There was no reason to."

"Is there any now?"

"Plenty."

"Such as?"

I was picking up courage and praying that I should not put my foot in my mouth in the process.

"Shut up, Thecla. A man may be wrong once in a while or wait for the most appropriate moment to do what he likes to do."

She looked at her brother. He was looking at the ground. She turned to my first wife. The Mother of Ache looked uneasy. She turned to me. I would not look at her.

"I – " she began and looked more puzzled.

"Thecla, listen when your husband is about to say something," I ordered, "and lacks correct words to put it in."

I raised my arms and held them wide open. Thecla got the message. She looked at me with raised eyebrows. Then she dropped her head like a ram ready to charge. When she raised it, there was a smile on her face.

In the twinkle of an eye, she dived into my arms. The

delicate scent of her perfume engulfed me. I drank it greedily and put my bloody arms round her. She put hers round me as if it was a thing we were accustomed to doing.

We held each other tight. Her arms were strong but tender. She was so soft and feminine. Her smooth cheek lay on mine and made me tipsy. My head was light with euphoria. My whole body was warm.

As if from far off, I heard "the Buffalo" and my voice saying "Thecla" immediately after.

After a long time during which we exchanged heart-warming breaths, she broke away from my embrace.

I looked at her with the greatest care in the world. For a while she also looked at me with her soft big round eyes.

Suddenly she did an unexpected thing. She dropped her head, covered her face with both hands and burst into tears.

I took a step towards her, fearing that I had inadvertently hurt her in some way.

"Thecla, what did I do wrong?"

She was weeping. Emotion shook her body as she tried to shake her head.

As if by consensus the rest of us let her shed more tears for some time. It calmed her down. After that I took her to task.

"What's the matter?" I asked. "If I have done anything wrong, tell me, please."

She took her hands from her face and smiled through her tears.

"I'm happy that my husband has come back home," she mumbled.

"Happy and crying?" Alemus asked.

The three of us burst into laughter.

"Yes," Thecla replied, "crying because Kang is no more with us. I shan't ever forget that and laughing because I still have him in the person of his identical twin brother, my present husband, the Father of Ache. I also laugh because I have such a good mbanya and a nice brother. So I'm crying in happiness."

Alemus shook his head.

"Women?" he declared shaking his head, "they cry when they are happy and laugh when they are sad. Father let them finish the cooking. My whole body is crying out for food."

The satisfaction that had seeped into my whole being had knocked out the urgent need of my body. I was starving and yet felt loaded with food. Thecla too looked sort of actively tired as she went in and out of the kitchen where she was working with her mbanya.

"I'm sure food'll soon be ready," I said to Alemus who sat there quiet, looking as if he had not noticed any odd occurrence in the courtyard, as if the world was still as it had been in the morning.

I too sat quiet because forced conversation would be a rude interruption of what was going on in our minds. Once in a while the noise of the loud pots and pans would reach us from the kitchen or a wisp warm hunger-provoking smell from the cooking food would go past us. Peace had settled in the Itung compound.

CHAPTER ELEVEN

The women finished cooking and served the food in expensive breakable plates that Thecla had brought from my upper house. The food was tasty. The stock had penetrated the coco yams and the meat was tender. Thecla had surely touched it up her way.

We all ate early supper together outside on the bamboo bench and two table chairs Thecla had also fetched from the living room for us the men. Each person had food on the thigh – the two women, the hunter, little Ache and I. It was a great occasion.

When we had finished eating, I went for the five litres of palm wine Alemus had brought. I gave the wine and my traditional cup made from the horn of a cow to the wine bringer to serve us the traditional way.

He put the wine on his right thigh, took my cup in his left hand and filled it by tilting the container downwards. I took this first cupful with my right hand and poured the contents ceremoniously on the ground for the ancestors.

I gave the cup back to Alemus who once more filled it and gave it to me. I took a sip from it and gave it back to him to drink for having carried the wine to its destination. He thrust his head back, put the cup to his lips and drank the wine in three big gulps. He smacked his lips with contentment.

He refilled the cup and gave it to me. I took a sip and

beckoned to the Mother of Ache. She bent over and came forward respectfully to take the cup in both hands. Still holding the cup in both hands, she emptied it and gave it back to Alemus to refill. That done, she took it from him and gave it to me.

It was now Thecla's turn. She did a little dance before she took her cup reverently from my hand. She drank the wine, had her brother refill the cup and, on bended knee, proffered the cup to me.

That woman! She was more versed in tradition than I had ever thought. I drank most of the wine in the cup and gave a little at the bottom to little Ache.

The Mother of Ache brought out three tall glasses from the cupboard in the living room. She gave one each to Alemus and Thecla and kept one for herself. I went on using my personal cup as owner of the compound. We drank freely and conversed in the ambience of our new found love and peace as a family.

Thecla sat opposite me but would not look at me directly. Her look reposed on everything else but my face. I was, however, keenly aware of her veiled scrutiny.

With a smile of satisfaction on her lips, the Mother of Ache sat beside her mbanya relaxed and holding her half glass of wine in her right hand. My whole life's happiness was in the hands of those two women.

With a smile of satisfaction on her lips, the Mother of Ache sat beside her mbanya on the same seat, holding her half glass of wine in her right hand. My whole life's happiness was in the hands of those two women.

All too soon, it was time to break up the party. The signal came from Alemus who wanted to get home before it was dark since the headlamp of his bicycle did not work.

Thecla put the chairs back into the living room while the

Mother of Ache washed the glasses they had just used. Little Ache caught Thecla's arm when she looked towards the upper house.

Big Ache picked up the now empty five-litre container for palm wine, greeted "his" father and the women politely and fetched his old bicycle near the wall of main door.

He strapped the container to the carriage of the bicycle while the rest of the group watched. Then he got onto his old machine and pedalled away with the chain cricking rhythmically.

Little Ache clung to Thecla's hand and began swinging her arm up and down.

"I am going with Auntie Thec," he declared with finality.

His mother looked at me.

"Let him go,'" I said. "For tonight only."

"No," my strong-willed son continued. "I'll be staying with her."

I saw an opening.

"Then what will you do when she comes to stay in this house?"

"I'll come back with her."

The answer served my purpose perfectly. Thecla stared at her clean feet. It is often said that silence is acceptance. The proof would be shown by her reaction to what I had decided to do.

I fetched a hind leg from the meat Alemus had left to smoke over the fire. Seemingly indifferently, I held it out to Thecla. Her mbanya and little Ache were watching her. She did not make any move to take the meat. She was staring at me in surprise.

"Take it!" cried little Ache. "You'll cook it for us tomorrow morning."

Thecla remained motionless. I put on an air of the lord and master.

"Thecla," I said in a contrived voice of great authority. "You know you're not allowed to keep your husband's arm suspended in the air!"

"I'm sorry," she said. "It's such a surprise."

My new wife took little Ache's hand in her left and with her right took the meat I was offering her. My heart glowed with joy. Thecla and her stepson walked slowly towards the upper house, holding the meat clumsily between them.

The rest of the party watched them in silence as if by plan. One person who had not taken part in the feasting was watching too. He had provided the meat. He was leaning in uninvolved satisfaction against a wall in my living room. It was the gun.

EPLILOGUE

Both my life and my mind are in a strange way today. Totally changed! Many are the moments when I want to put my right palm against my mouth and ululate like our women do when excited.

I am the richest man in our town and one of the richest in the country! Miracles have happened and there are more in stock. An odd conspiracy between my late brother and God Almighty made me see and consequently open the highway to achievements and bliss through my wife Thecla.

She is everything to me – mother of my second child, the second son who was born into indescribable fame, manager of all my businesses which she conceives and diligently runs, organiser and administrator of family matters and, despite all that, factotum of my whole compound.

Wuvet Itung, her first child was born with a veritable golden spoon in his mouth. He is in school in England. He succeeded to the Earldom of Snowdin whose defunct earl had been the foster father of my brother Kang.

He made Wuvet his heir in the absence of Kang. So an Itung is growing into the British House of Lords! My family goes to the U.K. at will and lives in unimaginable comfort.

Who would have thought I would one day mourn a foreigner so deeply not to talk of becoming family with him, not to talk of my thinking that he looked like my late father although he was a white man? The world changed and will keep changing till I meet Kang, his foster father and our parents.

I cannot tell the whole story here for the scope of the present narrative was not conceived to bear the details of what has only been lightly touched upon. These are in the book entitled "The Gun" which is making its way towards the publisher's, hopefully to be born some day.

About the Author

A pioneer student of Sacred Heart College after St. Joseph's School, Big Mankon, Richard C. Kumengisa was born in the Warders' Barracks at Up-Station, Mendankwe, Bamenda. He worked with the West Cameroon Public Service and attended the Universities of Yaounde and Paris (La Sorbonne), before taking up a teaching career.

His radio play "Singer of an old Song" won first prize in the 1996 environmental radio drama competition organised jointly by the British Council, Ministry of Environment and Forests, Living Earth and the BBC.

Author Contact:

C/O Mr. Yemen Chuba,
P.O. Box 5152, Nkwen-Bamenda,
North West Region, Cameroon.

+237676414409
+2376591567066
+237664433001

Email: kumengisab1@yahoo.com

Printed in the United States
By Bookmasters